PLASTIC FACES

MARTA ABROMAITYTE

VELOX BOOKS
Published by arrangement with the author.

CONTENT

911, WHAT IS YOUR EMERGENCY?

I've been in between jobs ever since I left college, doing different things here and there—odd jobs sometimes. It wasn't until I started as a 911 operator that I realised it's what I wanted to do for the rest of my life. The feeling that it gave me was indescribable; this warmth would wash over me like a cup of smooth, hot chocolate sliding down your throat and for a while, I was as happy as a clam.

I'd only been on the job about four months when I received one of the most chilling, unexplainable, and spine-tingling phone calls of my life. Now, I know what you're thinking. Most, if not all 911 calls are chilling or disturbing to a degree—of course they are. It's an emergency line. However, nearly all the calls can be explained, they can be *rationalised* and categorised. Nothing is left unclear or ambivalent. Rationality is what the human brain needs to be able to understand and comprehend a situation. When that's not possible, that's when you start to question everything you've ever known; everything you've ever accepted as reality.

The night it happened was a particularly gruelling shift, and I'd spent the last 10 hours just dispatching police for various domestics. I was about two hours from finishing when I received a call from a little girl called Samantha. The following is a transcript of that call.

***

Operator: Nine-one-one operator, what is your emergency?

Caller: Hello? Mummy's fallen over.

Operator: What's your name, honey?

Caller: Samantha.

Operator: Okay, Samantha. Can you tell me where you live?

Caller: I don't know the address. Can you find me?

Operator: Yes, I can trace the call, Samantha. Can you tell me what's happened?

Caller: Mummy's been acting all weird the past few days. Not sleeping at nights, going around scratching at things, scratching at walls. I'm always too scared to come out of my room. Tonight, I was in bed, and I started hearing this weird moaning sound. Mummy sounded like a zombie! *(giggle)*.

Operator: What's mummy doing right now, Samantha?

Caller: Mummy's on the floor right now. Won't get up.

Operator: Is mummy breathing, Samantha?

Caller: I don't know. I can't see her chest moving. I'm scared.

Operator: It's ok honey, help is on the way. I'll need you to stay on the line with me until they arrive. Can you do that?

Caller: Y-yes. Something's happening.

Operator: What's happening?

Caller: Mummy's twitching now. Her eyes are fluttering. Like a butterfly.

(In the background, distinct moaning sounds are heard and sounds of someone dragging themselves. Samantha is heard whimpering.)

Caller: Is someone coming? I'm scared.

Operator: Yes, Samantha. Help is not far away. What are those noises?

Caller: It's mummy.

Operator: What's mummy doing?

Caller: I'm hiding in my wardrobe. She is crawling on the floor, like a tarantula, and her eyes have gone all weird. She is hissing and this weird red foamy stuff is coming out of her mouth around the sides.

Operator: Can she see you?

Caller: I don't think she can see me yet. Is someone coming? Are they close?

Operator: Yes, very close.

Caller: (*whimpering*)

Operator: Samantha? Are you ok?

Caller: (*inaudible*)—mummy's walking backwards now. I think she knows where I am. Her black eyes are looking right at me. Please, I'm scared. Mummy wants to hurt me.

Operator: Samantha. What do you mean your mummy is walking backwards?

Caller: It's all upside down. Her legs are twisted the wrong way, her body is normal, but her head is all backwards too. You know when you twist your barbie's head? It's like that. She's shaking as she walks, kinda like a robot. She's coming.

Operator: Samantha, the police are right around the corner.

Caller: Mummy's smiling at me now. I think it's ok for me to come out.

Operator: Samantha, stay where you are.

Caller: Mummy? (*whimpering*)

Operator: Samantha? The police are right outside.

Caller: (*inaudible*) Mummy, please stop. You're scaring me.

Operator: Samantha?

Caller: I don't want to eat that Mummy. What do you mean it'll make me like you? Where are we going, Mummy?

A piercing scream is heard, and the line goes dead.

***

When the police arrived at the scene, they couldn't find Samantha nor her mother. In fact, the house didn't even look lived in. They reported that the lights didn't work, there was no furniture and in the middle of the living room, they found the decaying corpse of a dog. Looked to have been dead for weeks. Insects, maggots; all kinds of detestable things were found slithering around the house. No trace of any living human being was found.

I quit my job the very next morning. That call has haunted me to no end since; I just couldn't comprehend my experience. My boss and the police were all adamant that they were sent to the wrong address—it was all deemed to be the fault of the dispatcher. Me. But I know I wasn't wrong, I know the address was right and there was no error in the system, nor was it my fault.

I think about Samantha every day and pray that nothing bad happened to her, but deep in my heart, I know that creature that was pretending to be her mother did something unspeakable to her. Something unthinkable.

I'll never forget that scream.

BONE SOUP

It looked like an ordinary sign from a distance, there was nothing noteworthy or spectacular about it. It looked like one of those **'GOLD FOR CASH'** signs you sometimes see around Central London. It lacked any kind of creativity though; it was mind numbingly bland.

But as I kept seeing it again and again, something about it drew me in.

One evening, on my way home from work, I had decided to look closer. It was a quiet Autumn night, there was a biting chill in the air that predicted a frosty winter and I found myself feeling uneasy. As I edged closer, I realised it was the writing on the sign that had me unnerved.

REVOLUTIONARY BONE SOUP

COME AND TRY OUR VERY SPECIAL, VERY SENSATIONAL RECIPE! YOU WON'T REGRET IT. IT WILL CHANGE YOUR LIFE! 100% CUSTOMER SATISFACTION GUARANTEED.

GET YOURS HERE!

Follow the arrow and inquire within. Not for the faint hearted.

My interest was piqued. I had never seen something so unusual, so unbelievably *otherworldly* that I found myself following the arrow indicated at the bottom of the sign.

I walked for a few minutes until I came upon what looked like a pop-up shop. Its only distinctive feature was a dazzling neon sign that read **BONE SOUP** in bright, fluorescent letters.

I walked up to the door and saw there was no knob to turn. The shop looked abandoned, and I was beginning to doubt that any of this was actually real when suddenly a hatch opened and a bowl was thrust towards me.

It was covered by a small piece of fabric and on top lay a note which read:

TRY YOUR FIRST BONE SOUP ON US!

I picked up the bowl, sat down on the steps below, and removed the fabric.

The colour of the soup was a deep, dark brown. The texture was chunky and gooey, dripping off the spoon like thick, curdled milk. It smelled delicious, and I wanted nothing more than to feel the warm substance flow down my throat.

I swallowed it. It tasted wonderful, full of richness and flavour—I felt this unfathomable warmth inside of me. Until it started to burn.

My insides felt like they were on fire—the pain was blinding, searing, and I wanted to scream, but I couldn't. I looked down and saw that my body was *glowing*. I felt my skin melt away like candle wax, revealing the sinewy bone and tissue underneath. The pain surged through my body like lightning and with each and every breath, I felt my flesh pull apart like wet paper. The blood gushed out of me like a fountain, staining the asphalt beneath a ruby red. The raw and exposed flesh fell away like cooked meat, and I saw my lower half dissolving—leaking into the bowl.

Before everything went black, I saw a gnarled, moistened, and fleshy arm extend from within the hatch and snatch the bowl back inside.

MY FRIEND JACK

I've known Jack for a good 5 or 10 years. We went to school together, went to college together and at one point we even fucked the same girl... together. Anyhow, that's not important right now. The point I was trying to make is that Jack and I were close, the best of friends. Jack got married at 20, had a kid at 24 and pretty much forgot I existed after that, but I didn't blame him really—I was still stuck in the past, thinking of myself as some sort of cool and edgy bachelor. When in reality, I was nothing, but a grade A fuck up. Jack grew up. I didn't.

Jack and I lost touch for a few years, only the obligatory 'Merry Christmas' and 'Happy Birthday' when the time came. The one thing Jack and I have always had in common is our mutual love for vintage records, vinyl in particular. I, for one, salivated for them and Jack was pretty into them too. It's the one thing that tethered us together all these years, despite the familial obligations (for Jack) and the crippling loneliness (for me).

Recently, Jack emailed me about a rare record he had found. It's the first correspondence from him I'd had in literally *months*. He was so excited too and so was I, not only about the prospect of some rare record he'd found, but I was happy just to *hear* from him. It was normal conversation at first but after a while the emails became... frantic, delusional almost.

***

From: Jackyboy@xxxx.com
To: Matt123@xxxx.com
SUBJECT: Record

Hey Matt! Man, it's been too long, huh? Sorry I haven't been in touch for a while. You know how it is. Maya has just turned 2, the terrible twos. I barely get any sleep nowadays. Janet and I are in a bad place now. We don't talk. We sleep in different beds. It's fucked. I think a divorce is on the cards. Anyway, enough about me. The reason I'm getting in touch is because I found something really fucking cool that I wanted to tell you about.

I found this record in an old thrift store, ancient. Mint condition. I don't even know why I looked at it or how I found it, but it just caught my eye. It didn't even have a name, but something about it really drew me in. I'm going to give it a listen tonight but just wanted to touch base with you since it's been way too long, man.

I'll let you know what it's like!

Jack.

***

From Jackyboy@xxxx.com
To Matt123@xxxx.com
SUBJECT: This record is fucking weird.

Hey Matt, it was nice to hear from you too! So, this is fucked, but I listened to the record, and it has really messed me up. There was nothing particularly spectacular about it, it was a bit dull if anything, but it's what happened *after* that I am having trouble understanding.

I waited until both Maya and Janet were asleep, and I played the record in my study. The melody was sweet and sombre but at the same time, there was something eerie about it. There were no breaks in song, just the same tune over and over. You know the other fucked up thing? I've been hearing it ever since. I can't make out whether it's all in my head or I am *actually* hearing it.

I've been seeing these horrible things too. It doesn't matter if I am awake or asleep; the images are unrelenting. I can't even bear to utter them here, to you.

Call me.

Jack.

***

From Jackyboy@xxxx.com
To Matt123@xxxx.com
SUBJECT: The blood??!!!!

Matt, the blood. There is fucking blood everywhere. It covers the walls and the body of my sleeping wife; she looks so peaceful. I can even see it when they're all awake; walking around, lathered in crimson. Janet says I've really lost my shit, but I can *see* it. I can even smell it in the air—the moist, metallic scent lingers.

My daughter Matt. Maya. I keep seeing her detached, crudely severed head; it follows me wherever I go. Her blood-stained teeth chatter and her tongue writhes in her impossibly wide mouth. She torments me as I try to sleep, as I try to piss, as I try and do *anything*. Her fucked up floating head is always there. I don't know what to do anymore.

Please call me.

Jack.

***

From Jackyboy@xxxx.com
To Matt123@xxxx.com
SUBJECT: I think I'm in hell.

Matt, this isn't funny anymore. I thought you were supposed to be my friend?! Why have you been outside my house? What the fuck do you think you're playing at? Where are you? You haven't been returning my calls and my emails have been bouncing back. Why aren't you answering me. Please, I need you, I need someone.

The music won't leave me alone now. I can hear it every hour of every fucking day and I can't take it anymore. My family isn't my family anymore. My life isn't my life anymore. Janet has been skulking around the house like the walking dead; staring into the walls, scratching at them. I've tried to stop her but that isn't her anymore. Whatever this is, it has taken my family.

Her eyes are hollow and inside, her heart is black.

The weeping is getting worse. I can hear the tortured voices as I sit here typing this. Please help me, Matt. This vinyl, I think it's a live recording of hell.

It's been 72 hours and the sun hasn't set.

Jack.

***

From Jackyboy@xxxx.com
To Matt123@xxxx.com
SUBJECT: Maya.

Everything around me is black. I am surrounded by the decaying corpses of my wife and daughter; they aren't dead though. It all keeps repeating—I have lived the same day repeatedly for weeks. I wake up, the music follows me, and my wife and child are alive again. Then they die and my world is fire.

Have you been outside again? I don't know anymore; everything looks the same. I have tried going outside, but it's just darkness out there—I don't think I'm in Kansas anymore. There are carved up bodies everywhere, I don't even know who they are. I think I saw you out there, Matt. Did it get you? I'm so sorry.

The fire is closing in around me; I don't think I have long left.

Please, Matt. Forgive me.

Jack.

***

After that, the emails ceased. I tried to get in contact with him, but the phone went unanswered. I tried Janet's phone and that, too, yielded no results. The horrifying thing was, is that I tried to respond to his emails, I really did. I sent him frantic notes back, but it was as if they never reached him.

I contacted the police, but apparently, when they arrived at Jack's address, they found the house empty. *"Went on vacation,"* they told me. I tried to show them the emails, but they wouldn't listen, citing me a lunatic. I knew I wasn't a crazy person, though, and neither was Jack. He discovered a gateway to something unspeakable, something *evil* and it took him, took his family.

A few days ago, I received something in the post. It was a round package; perfectly wrapped. It didn't take me long to figure out what was inside. It was the record. There was no return address.

The fear has been gnawing at me ever since I touched it but there was something else mixed in with that fear too. *Curiosity.*

I'm too scared to listen to it but I don't know if I can stop myself.

PLEASE DON'T LOOK

I absentmindedly flicked the switch to turn off my computer monitor, it was 5:30pm, and I was finally done for the day. I couldn't wait to get out of there—it was Friday, and I was eager for the weekend. Yearning to wind down and forget about work for a day or two. I worked for a publishing house called Raven Mill Books as an Editorial Assistant—a lifelong dream of mine. I spent most of my day reading. Granted, the stories aren't always compelling, but hey, I still loved immersing myself in the work of others, whatever it may be.

I turned to face Patricia, the girl that always sat next to me—I think she was in marketing. I was never sure, and she wasn't very talkative.

"I'm done for the day, see you Monday." I said, picking up my handbag.

My bag fell from my weak grasp as I glimpsed her face. She had this permanent grimace that seemed to be fixed to her features. Her mouth was twisted, as if she was in pain, and the colour of her flesh was that of pure snow. It was as if someone had sculpted her face to be in a perpetual state of fear. But it was her eyes that chilled the blood in my veins. They were a deep, dark red, like two little scarlet ruby diamonds, and I could see tiny droplets forming on the edge of her damp eyelashes—tears.

I had never seen fear like it. It was overwhelming. It terrified me.

"Pat?" I said meekly.

She was so still, so silent—an unmoving statue. I touched her arm, and it was cold, hard and rigid—if I didn't know better and if it weren't for the distorted expression that lined her face, I'd think she was dead. *She was looking at something on her screen.* Something that was making her look and act this way. I tore my gaze away from her ghostly face and directed it toward her screen. It was blank, nothing but white noise and static. *What in the hell was she looking at?* I wondered to myself.

I stood up, hoping to call someone. Anyone. This wasn't normal, I knew that. Perhaps Pat had suffered some sort of breakdown? That thought had crossed my mind. But then I would remember her face and the fear would grip me tighter than ever. *Something wasn't right.* When I scanned the room, I nearly passed out.

They were all just sitting there—faces glued to their screens with wet and bleeding eyes. *Every single one of them.* I saw my friend Triss, over in Sales and her boss Miranda. All wide-eyed and unblinking. I saw Ursula, Ruby, Nathan and Tom—all my friends, everyone I knew. Every single one staring at their computer screens. I walked toward Triss, my eyes filling with tears.

"Triss?"

The room was so quiet, so completely still that I could hear my own heartbeat in my ears—beating incessantly. It was deafening.

Triss didn't respond, didn't even flinch. Just continued to sit and stare at her screen, eyes ruby red and weeping. As I neared, I noticed her trembling, ever so slightly—the fear just radiating off her body. She was *glowing*, almost. My hand reached out to touch her auburn hair—it felt dry to the touch, hardened. As if someone had poured wax all over it. My hand travelled down to her shoulder. I prodded it gently. No response.

I'd just about had enough, so I spun her chair around so that she faced me.

"Triss. Snap the fuck out of it." I said, shaking her.

I stared into her glassy eyes and saw my own horrified face reflected in them. At that moment, she began convulsing violently, her body shook with a fervour I had never seen before. Her bloodshot eyes rolled back into her head, glistening in the pale evening light as she shook. I loosened my grip and stood, watching in horror.

I fumbled for my phone, desperate to call the police and the ambulance—the whole fucking cavalry. I attempted to dial 999, but my heart sank when I saw that there was no reception—no fucking signal. My phone lay, defeated in my sweated palm. I looked at the quivering body of Triss and my eyes widened in horror as I watched her *change*, morph into something entirely different. Her convulsions had worsened, and she had fallen to the floor. Her mouth was grotesquely askew, white foam dribbled from the sides. I could see her veins, they were thick and bulging—a deep, overpowering red. I saw them quiver as the blood coursed through them. Then she screamed—her mouth opened unbelievably wide and within I saw that she had bitten her tongue nearly in half. I felt powerless. All I could do was sit there and watch her die from whatever the fuck was happening around me. Her veins continued to swell, growing ever bigger and before I could blink—they *exploded*.

Before she succumbed, I heard her whisper something. Something that sent shivers down my spine.

"Mum, please."

I didn't know why those words escaped her dying mouth. Why was she begging? Triss' mum had been dead for three years. She died in a car accident, was impaled by a fucking truck apparently—it was macabre.

Before Triss' blood had a chance to dry on my brow, Miranda caught my attention. She was concealed behind her screen so I couldn't see her properly, but I could see the top of her head from where I was standing. Something about her shrouded demeanour frightened me even more. I knew what she was doing, of course—I already knew she was glued to her screen like everyone else, but it was what I could *hear* that sent spikes though my heart.

She was fucking laughing.

I observed her head move up and down like a bobbing apple. I got to my feet, slowly—with my eyes closed. Believe it or not, I was too scared to look. When I eventually opened them, I let out this inhuman howl that I am certain was not my voice. Miranda's face was a ghastly, terrifying sight. Her eyes were unmoving, unblinking—just like the rest of them but there was something strange and different about her mouth. She was *smiling*. A wide, unearthly smile that spread from ear to ear. Tears streamed down her face; I could see the dread in her eyes. Why was she smiling? Laughing even? I didn't know and I don't think I wanted to know.

"Miranda?" I didn't know what else to say.

She didn't answer me, of course. Just continued to stare at the nothingness on her screen, laughing quietly, her body trembling. Her laugh grew louder and louder with each passing minute. It was unnatural—like a witch's cackle. It was as if she couldn't catch her breath with each bout of ever-increasing laughter. It was downright creepy. She wouldn't stop—her laugh became deep, guttural and dry. As if her throat was parched, as dry as a bone. Then she began choking; hands clawing at her throat. Still, she never once shifted her gaze away from her screen.

In between fits of suffocation, she managed to say something.

"Phillip, why are you doing this to me?"

I didn't know Miranda well, so I had no clue who Phillip was. Her head fell, hitting her desk with a bang—I heard her skull crack.

I was fucking done. I had to get out of there. I rushed downstairs, but when I got there, I realised that I couldn't leave—the doors were sealed shut. I screamed until my voice was hoarse and throat was sore—freedom was just metres away from me but whatever was happening in this building, it didn't want me to leave. I *couldn't* leave. Why was I the only one that didn't get affected? I turned my screen off before everyone else, I was sure of that. So, it was pure, dumb luck.

That was when I saw something pale and gangling just out of the corner of my eye, just out of reach. It moved so swiftly I was sure it was a trick of the light, but it petrified me even more because I *knew* that wasn't true. *Something* was there, lurking, dwelling in the dark corners of the office. Always just out of reach. I felt like I was being watched.

Not knowing what else to do, I made my way back to the main desks—I could go nowhere else. When I walked back in, the sight that greeted me was beyond words, *beyond* anything normal. Every single person in the room was lying face down, face hugging their keyboards. Their heads, oh my god, their heads. They were all shrivelled, like those perfectly preserved shrunken human heads that are used for grotesque rituals. It looked like they had been left out in the sun for too long; all desiccated. The skin was far too tight—the colour a dirty brown, mummified.

Their eyes were sunken, practically non-existent. A slimy, luminous liquid trickled out of their open mouths.

I had sunk to the floor, feeling so helpless—the tears falling like raindrops from my tired eyes. What was I to do? Then I heard a voice, a voice that I hadn't heard in 10 years.

"You'll be okay, Delcie. I'm here for you."

It was the voice of my brother, Timothy.

Timothy has been dead for 10 years.

I covered my ears. "Please, leave me alone."

"I can't do that, Delcie. You need to come and look at me. SEE ME!"

It sounded like my brother, only I knew that it wasn't. I was suddenly overwhelmed by this feeling I couldn't describe that I didn't recognise. It was a terrifying craving. I wanted to see Timothy. I longed to see him.

"Tim, is it really you?" I said, my own voice sounding so alien to me.

"It's me, Delcie. Come to me."

I saw the hideous shadows again; they had multiplied. Lurking in the corners, dancing in the shadows. They were getting *closer* now.

Before I could stop myself, I got up and, like a robot, walked toward my computer screen. Nothing else mattered now. My brother's voice whizzed like a rollercoaster in my frazzled mind, so quiet and yet so convincing. I knew what I had to do. I just didn't know if I could do it.

***

I'm sitting by my computer screen now—I haven't turned it on yet. I don't know what time it is. What I do know, is that everyone around me is dead. I still can't get out and I still can't call the police. I'm writing this on my phone because I want there to be a record of what's happened here today, just in case I don't make it. There is only one thing left for me to do, I know that now. I realise it and I feel it in my heart, pulsating like a tumour.

The only way out is to *look.*

THE PLANT

I remember the day I first noticed it. Its green bulbous stems protruded at odd angles—angles that *shouldn't* have been possible, and yet they were. I had never seen a plant like that before. *Was it even a plant?* I had no recollection of planting it and couldn't figure out where it came from. It just appeared one day—much like a cancerous cyst. I eyed its curious stalks—the colour a deep and menacing red. The moist sap dribbled onto the blackened earth, forming a puddle that reflected the morning sun. It glistened so brightly that it hurt my eyes.

I wanted to approach it, observe it up close, but every time I tried, I'd feel this crippling anxiety that gripped me so tightly that I found it hard to breathe. I needed to get rid of it—something told me that it shouldn't be there. I felt foolish. It was just a plant, wasn't it? Albeit a peculiar looking one, but nothing more than a plant. I tried to tell myself this.

I armed myself with a pair of large shears, gripping them tightly—as irrational as this may sound, I hoped that they would protect me, hoped that they would serve as armour. I couldn't explain why. Something about this curious plant petrified me.

I stepped outside; the wind chilled the sweat that had formed on my brow. With caution, I took a step forward—as if I was approaching a bomb that could go off any second. As I neared, the fear that had enveloped me tightened its grip—my breathing became erratic and my heartbeat like a drum. I tried to shake it off. *It's just a plant*, I kept repeating that to myself over and over, hoping it would stifle this unfounded dread. For a moment, it did.

I took a deep breath and moved even closer. That's when the smell hit me. It was putrid and hot, hanging in the air like a decaying corpse. I pinched my nose tight, but the acrid scent still trickled through—like thick and balmy oil. I could feel bile rising in the back of my throat. With watery eyes, I watched the plant swaying gently in the soft breeze. With each motion, the smell intensified.

I lifted the shears with all the strength that I could muster and with one swift movement, I severed it at its stalk. The stem fell to the ground, and I could have sworn I felt the earth below my feet tremble. I took a deep breath, filling my lungs with air. The air felt so much lighter, cleaner. I exhaled, feeling relief—I felt weightless suddenly, as if I'd been carrying bags full of wet, putrescent planks upon my back. I hadn't noticed the drastic change until I'd severed its gnarled stalk.

***

The next day I woke up feeling fatigued, my body felt heavy; gluey and entirely unlike my own. I walked with legs that felt like thin planks of wood; hard and flimsy. When I reached my kitchen window, I found myself feeling faint at the sight that greeted me.

It was the plant.

It was back and more grotesque than ever. It stood tall, as tall as me—in fact, it was exactly my height. Its bulbous shape pulsated in the hot sun—it was almost *smouldering*. I could see smoke emanating from its crooked stalks. The leaves glistened as if doused in fuel. I could almost smell it.

I looked down at the blackened earth and saw its roots throbbing and warping, stirring the dirt that surrounded it. It moved closer.

It beckoned to me. I pleaded with it.

"No, please. I don't want to."

My voice sounded gritty, as if my vocal cords had been shredded.

I was no longer in control of my own body and found myself walking toward the plant. I tried to scream, but no sound came out. My throat felt raw, my mouth wet. I touched my face and glanced at my fingertips—they were covered in soil; damp and coarse. I looked down and saw that my body was caked in blackened earth, as if I'd been buried alive. I didn't know what was happening to me.

As I neared the plant, my vision became blurry, and I passed out.

***

When I awoke, I saw my kitchen window. I was in my garden, upright, but I couldn't turn my head to look around. I tried to move my arms, but I found that I couldn't *feel* anything—the sensation of my limbs was absent. I could feel the panic rising within me, threatening to erupt like a violent volcano. That was when I saw *her.* She was standing by her window, eyeing me curiously. She began moving toward the door, slowly. In her hand she held a large pair of shears, the same shears that I know I owned.

She was exactly my height.

THE BATHROOM

It was Christmas Eve and Oxford Street was a steady hum of noise—the streets were buzzing like angry bees. The skies were a sea of gloom, but the bright, shimmering Christmas lights gave the grey asphalt an ethereal glow; like something out of The Lord of The Rings. It was a beautiful evening, considering.

My head felt a little fuzzy and the voices of the people I passed sounded far away—muffled. It felt like someone had stuffed my ears full of cotton wool. I felt drunk, but I didn't remember drinking any alcohol. I glanced at my watch; it was 9.30pm. How did it get so late? Wasn't I just at work? My head felt heavy, and I struggled to recall what I did the past three and a half hours. Nothing seemed right. Everything around me was too bright, too *sharp*, like I was drifting through a dream. I pushed the feelings of incongruity aside and continued on. I needed to get home.

As I walked, the lights danced in front of my eyes like elegant ballerinas and I watched the brightness blur and warp in the dim evening light, willing my eyes to focus.

I felt my bladder spasm and knew that I couldn't continue my tedious journey home without first finding a toilet. I scanned my immediate surroundings and, to my dismay, found that I was surrounded by nothing but retail stores. I groaned. There had to be a toilet *somewhere*. At times it felt like the city was a concrete maze from which there was no escape, especially when you were most desperate to do just that. I hurried past the distinct and yet bland, colourless buildings—a stark contrast to how warm and inviting they looked just a mere few hours before. My bladder was ready to burst at that point, and that's when I saw it.

The toilet.

It was situated between Primark and Topshop—a ramshackle wooden hut nestled between the brickwork like it was the most natural thing in the world. Dumbfounded, I approached it. It struck me how oddly placed this toilet was. Who would put a wooden cabin in the middle of a busy London Street? It wasn't possible. I'd walked this street thousands of times. This toilet didn't exist. It *shouldn't* exist. It made no fucking sense.

My stomach twisted into knots; my insides felt like scrambled eggs—gooey and soft. As if someone had whipped my organs with a rusted fork. I didn't want to go in—something about the rotten, dripping wood didn't feel right, but my bladder was throbbing, and the pain was beginning to feel unbearable.

I took another, albeit tentative, step forward. I could feel the fear and anticipation surge through me like lightning. I turned my head to look behind me and saw the street was empty, only a few bodies left wandering—none paying any attention to me nor this bizarrely placed toilet. I felt queasy and on edge. You know that feeling of impending doom you're apparently supposed to get right before a heart attack strikes? That was how I felt.

My bladder spasmed once more, and I knew that I couldn't hold it in any longer. I rushed in and ran to the nearest cubicle—barely paying any attention to my surroundings. I sat down and felt the relief wash over me, closing my eyes for just a moment. When I opened them again, I saw a crack in the door that revealed a small hole. My heart almost leaped into my mouth when I saw someone peering at me.

It was a woman.

She had the most detestable smile I had ever seen, a maniacal grin stretching from ear to ear. Her gnarly, crooked teeth exposed, the colour of aged oatmeal. Her skin hung loose like thin and dampened parchment paper, like someone had peeled it off and reattached it crudely using glue. She looked at me, her eyes sunken into their sockets—swollen and bloodshot. She was repulsive.

I was frozen to the spot, utterly petrified and unable to move a muscle. The silence was deafening, I couldn't hear anything but my own shallow breathing. It didn't last long, though—my blood ran cold when I heard a small, quiet chuckle. I forced myself to look at her once more and I was horrified by what I saw. Her loathsome smirk hadn't wavered, her mouth barely twitched, but her shoulders were moving up and down ever so slightly. *She was fucking laughing.* It made my skin crawl and I could feel this cavernous pit forming inside of me.

"W-what do you want?" I managed to stutter.

She didn't answer me. Just continued staring and smiling. I didn't know how much time had passed—all I wanted to do was get out of there, I just didn't know how. I sat there with my trousers around my ankles, wracking my useless brain for ideas, when suddenly, the withered crone lifted her finger and pointed it at me. It was long, gnarly, and skeletal with a crooked nail hanging on at the end. Then she spoke.

"Only the damned find this place."

Her voice was guttural and croaky, very much akin to a smoker. Her chest wheezed as she spoke. When she opened her mouth, specks of dust escaped and swirled in the air as if her mouth had been sewn shut for a decade. Despite this, her smile never wavered—her eyes burned into mine as I sat quivering.

"W-w-what do you want?" I asked, barely hearing my own voice.

Her smile grew even wider. I could see the flesh at the sides of her mouth splitting and cracking, blood began to dribble down her chin—she flicked her tongue out like a serpent and licked it up.

"You know why you're here." She said, rotating her leathery finger as she spoke.

"I-I-I don't know. Please let me go."

She shook her head.

"Only the damned find this place."

"Only the damned find me."

I shook my head. This wasn't happening.

"No. No, you can't take me. This isn't fucking real," I said.

"I already have," she said, baring her teeth at me like a rabid dog.

Then, in a blink of an eye, she vanished.

I scrambled to my feet and ran for the door. I needed to get the fuck out of there. When I opened the door, though, I saw nothing but blackness—a deep, impenetrable darkness that I never knew existed. I didn't want to go in, but I needed to leave that place. I took a step forward and walked through.

Nothing happened for a while, and I couldn't see—I felt blind. Then I saw something ahead, a light; yellow in tone, it looked warm and inviting. I ran towards it, viewing it as my salvation, my freedom. The closer I got, the brighter the light became. I couldn't understand—the exit should have been right here; I should have been on the high street moments ago. I continued on and my heart sank when I realised where it was leading me to.

Back to that bathroom.

I felt utter despair; panic bubbled up inside of me. *What the fuck was happening?* I went around in a circle somehow and ended up right back where I started. I turned around and through the blackness, I saw the same yellow light behind me. There was no escape. I didn't know what to do. Then I heard her voice.

"Only the damned..."

Was I damned? I suddenly couldn't remember what I did before I got there. It was the same peculiar feeling I experienced before I found this toilet, that feeling of fear and unfamiliarity. *I couldn't remember anything.* What did I do this morning? What was my job for a living? I tried to grasp at the memories, like drowning kittens gasping for air, but with every attempt, the memories faded. It was like trying to look through fog or trying to solve a puzzle you know you never can.

"There is nowhere to go now, Cassandra."

"It's over."

In the darkness, I saw a silhouette. It was her; I knew it was her. I couldn't see clearly, but deep in my heart, I knew. Her lanky, grotesque frame was visible against the glaring light of the bathroom stall—her spindly arms hung at her sides, nails as long and as sharp as knives. Her straw-like hair stuck out at all angles, unbrushed and unkempt. I couldn't see her face, but I knew that she was smiling. I knew that she was here for me and I for her.

"Come to me Cassandra."

That's what I did then, I went to her.

***

The memories flashed in my head like the reels on an old movie tape. I remembered crying. I remembered Timothy standing over me, he was talking, his mouth moved, but I couldn't quite hear what he was saying. Then it dawned on me. He didn't love me anymore; he was sorry but there was someone else.

I remembered feeling this blind rage, my insides burned like a hot flame; it enveloped my heart. I remembered seeing the knife, and I remembered how it felt when I slid the knife into his flesh; it was effortless, splitting apart like butter. He pleaded with me, but I didn't care, I couldn't feel anything but the burning flame inside of me. I sliced his flesh until there was nothing left, until the floor was nothing but a sea of ruby red. I carved into him until he was dead.

I looked down, and I screamed, I screamed until my throat was raw, but it was too late. I brought the knife down to my wrist and knew that I had no other choice.

***

Tears streamed down my face as I approached her. I knew I deserved this, I deserved to be here for what I did.

As I neared, she opened her arms in an embrace, and within, I saw thousands of them—others like me. They writhed and thrashed amidst the flames. I watched as their flesh melted and dripped like candle wax, leaving them bare, red and raw. I watched as their faces dissolved, revealing the tender muscle, bone, and viscera underneath. They were being skinned and burned alive, over and over. This was their punishment. Just as it was about to become mine.

THE TOOTHMAN CHRONICLES

I was brushing my teeth the first time I saw him. I thought it was the way the light reflected off my teeth at first or a simple trick of the mind—a hallucination, if you will. But when I saw him, again and again; I knew that he was real. The Toothman. Elusive as he was, he would always surprise me when I least expected him. A little wink of a weary eye here, a little wiggle of the fingers there.

It started after I visited the dentist and for the longest time, I believed that he put the Toothman in there. Is that something that dentists do? Put strange little men inside your mouth? No, that's fucking stupid. Has to be. Maybe it's just one of those things— he's always been there. I just haven't noticed him, you know?

Maybe, the Toothman is in us all. Sitting there among your pearly whites, twiddling his many thumbs, biding his time; just waiting for the right moment to make you question everything you've ever known. Reality has been skewed ever since I started seeing him and I could swear that he's been getting bigger. Like a new-born baby, moulding and sculpting himself into shape.

My tooth has been on fire lately, I know it's him doing it. I've *seen* him take his long claws that I thought used to be hands to the nerves of my tooth, stabbing and slashing. The little shit thinks he can carve me from the inside out.

When I looked in the mirror, he would laugh maniacally and wave at me—the deranged prick. He grew so big that he almost covered my whole cheek and he started to leave me little messages, little warnings, you know. It always started with an overwhelming stinging, like someone was biting the inside of my cheek. I don't know that it hurt. I think it did, but I couldn't be sure. The Tooth-man has a peculiar way of distorting and warping your mind.

So, I took a pair of pliers to my teeth, and I pulled them all out, one by one. Hoping to extract him, like a pesky thorn. If you've ever had to pull out your own tooth because of the Tooth-man, then you are familiar with the blinding, razor-sharp pain. It didn't work, though. He was still there, you see. The reason I knew is because when I looked inside my mouth, I could see his beady eyes blinking at the back of my mouth.

I was asleep one night when my throat was slit open, it unrav-elled like the seams on a frayed shirt. I tried to cry out, but my mouth quickly filled with blood. I watched as the Toothman's clawed hand emerged out of the cherry-red crevice. It was covered in viscera and tangled in my blood vessels. I felt the rest of my body unwrap, like a Christmas present.

The Toothman stepped out. He turned to me, whispering; *"Thanks for accommodating me, big fella"*.

I tried to smile; they grow up so fast.

THE BODY

I woke up next to a dead body, and it had no face.

It was the body of a man—at least I think it was a man. His hair glistened in the bright morning sun; the colour as black as night. His skin was pearl white, as smooth as silk—it had an almost plastic sheen to it. He looked like a porcelain doll. I know that's really morbid—to be describing the appearance of a dead man, but I couldn't stop staring at him. My eyes travelled over his pristine frame. It looked like he was asleep—if it wasn't for the fact that he had no fucking face.

The flesh that covered his featureless face was immaculate, snowy in appearance. Not a single blemish or imperfection lined the pink skin. I wanted to reach out and touch it, feel its glossiness under my rough fingertips, but I didn't dare. As I stood and stared, in complete awe and horror—I found myself wondering how it felt. I had always thought that dead bodies were rigid and stiff—rigor mortis and all that, but this man looked gooey, his skin squidgy and plump. His limbs were relaxed, loose almost. *How fucking fresh is he?* I asked myself, terrified.

I had no idea where he came from, but his presence in my dingy, dust covered flat unnerved me. This horrifying, ghastly looking corpse had no place here.

The first thing I did was call the police, of course. I did briefly wonder if perhaps they would deem me a lunatic or some crazed maniac, but I knew I didn't kill him and I sure as hell couldn't make his face disappear so as outlandish as the whole situation would appear, I just wanted someone else to see what I was seeing. To reassure me that I hadn't gone mad.

I paced back and forth as I waited for them to arrive—glancing briefly at the splayed remains on my ruffled bed sheets. My mind began to wonder, asking questions I knew I didn't have the answers to. *Who put him there?*, *Where did he come from?*, *Where was his fucking face!?*. These questions burned hot in my mind like an open fire and as much as I tried to rationalise it all to myself—I knew it was futile. There was no logical explanation for this.

I found myself sweating profusely. I wanted to appear normal, calm, and *self-assured,* but despite my best efforts, I knew I looked nervous and jittery. I caught a glimpse of myself in my hallway mirror and I looked downright fucking *deranged.* I tried to compose myself, telling myself to breathe—to calm down, but it was impossible. It's not every day you wake up next to a dead man with no face. That was something I was certain of.

The sudden knock on my door brought me back to reality—I clutched at my chest, attempting to keep my heart from bursting out. It was beating incessantly. I had no idea why I was so worried. I walked toward my front door, suddenly immobilised by this fear I didn't recognise. The knocking intensified.

"Hello? Police, can you open the door?" The voice sounded gruff and deep, thumping across my flat like the waves on a stormy ocean. Hesitantly, my hand reached out. Time felt like it was moving painfully slow—each minute felt like an eternity. I wiped the sweat that had formed on my bushy brow and turned the handle. The outside breeze chilled my clammy skin, and I found myself forcing a smile—I had to look normal.

"Hello?" I said. My voice sounded quiet, muffled, as if I had been submerged under water. In front of me stood two police officers—a man and a woman.

"Mr Ghustov? Arthur Ghustov?" One of them spoke, it was the man. He looked sombre, like he meant business. He smiled, at least I think it was a smile, but it was difficult to perceive—his eyes were cold; unfriendly. His lips were spread thin across his face—his teeth barely visible. He stood tall, much taller than the woman beside him. My eyes travelled towards her instead, she looked kinder.

She looked more welcoming, inviting—my guess was that she was the good cop. She smiled at me. Her smile was tender, *reassuring*, revealing a row of pristine white teeth. I suddenly felt much lighter and felt my heart slow to a normal rhythm.

"Hi Mr Ghustov. I'm PC Johnson and this is PC Spade. You called?" She said, taking a step into my flat. I guessed they didn't need an invite.

"Er, yes, yes, I did. This is probably going to sound very strange but... I... er... woke up next to a dead body this morning." I said.

They both stood, aghast, unsure of what to say for a split second. The bad cop spoke first. PC Spade, I think his name was.

"Did you just say you woke up next to a dead body?"

"Y-y-yes, yes, that's right." I could feel my heart begin to race, pounding against my chest like the wings of a hummingbird. I ran my hands through my hair, my palms came away moistened, as if I'd run them under a tap. The nerves were getting to me again.

"Just stay where you are please, Mr Ghustov." Said the good cop, her hand reaching for the black baton stowed in her belt.

My immediate reaction was to put my hands up, I wasn't sure why. Perhaps I'd watched too many cop shows—this was the UK, not the US, but I was petrified. I was innocent. I opened my mouth to speak, to defend myself, but the bad cop raised his gloved hand, a stern look enveloping his face and I immediately knew it was in my best interests to shut up.

They both slowly walked into my bedroom, and I waited, with my hands in the air, expecting for the cuffs to enclose around my wrists at any moment.

"Is this some kind of joke?" It was the voice of the good cop.

"Mr Ghustov? Get in here." The man's voice carried across my hallway, slicing the silence like a butcher slices into the flesh of a slaughtered lamb.

Tentatively, I walked towards my bedroom. When I walked in, my blood ran cold.

The bed was empty.

There was not a single trace of the body. It was as if it never existed. I began questioning everything I saw that morning. I looked at both police officers. A mixture of disdain, disgust, and exasperation lined their faces.

"Care to explain, Mr Ghustov? We don't take kindly to false reports." Said PC Johnson, her kind eyes were no longer kind.

It felt as if I had suddenly gone mute, I couldn't find the words, couldn't conjure any kind of explanation for what had happened.

"I-I-I swear it was here. Why would I lie about something like this?" Was all I could manage.

"We'll let you off with a warning this time, Mr Ghustov, but waste police time again and we won't hesitate to arrest you for making false reports." The voice of the bad cop, PC Spade, was wrathful, and it terrified me.

I wanted to beg them to believe me, implore them to help me, but before I could say anything, they hurried out of the door.

There was no explanation for the body appearing and there was no explanation for the body disappearing, either. It was ludicrous. Maybe I had gone mad after all. Or maybe it had all been a dream. There is such a thing, isn't there? I think it's called lucid dreaming or something. Where you're so convinced that what's happening around you is real, but it isn't, and you wake up. I was waiting for that moment; I was waiting to wake up.

But that moment never came and the next day, the body was there again.

This time, though, it was a little different—not as fresh, not as *clean,* and pristine as it was the previous day. I observed the skin and noticed that it looked taut, threatening to rip and tear like sodden tissue. The limbs and stomach looked swollen, bloated and hard, on the verge of rupture. The colour of the skin was a deep purple, as if the body had been beaten repeatedly. The smell of death lingered in the air like cigarette smoke, transmitting its putrid scent across the room as it moved invisible and unseen.

I'm no expert on body decomposition so I couldn't comment on the stage of decay, however, judging by the rancid smell, I would say stage fucking stench. If I wasn't so shocked and terri-fied, I would have probably thrown up—that's what a normal person would do when exposed to something so grisly. But what was happening here was so much more grotesque than simply finding a dead body. There was so much more terror yet to come.

I knew that calling the police again was futile, because he dis-appeared just as quickly as he did the first time. I knew he would be back the next day though, and I knew there was nothing I could do about it.

Somehow, I could feel deep in my bones that he was here to show me something. I just wasn't sure what it was yet.

***

When he first appeared, he had no face; there was nothing but a smooth surface where his features should have been. After a few days, I could see some forming—two small indentations where the eyes would be, a protruding lump that looked somewhat like a nose and finally, a thin, long slit that I assumed was his mouth.

I couldn't explain it, but with each passing day, his facial features would materialise, becoming clearer and clearer, while the rest of him festered and disintegrated from decay. His body was blackened and soiled; I was beginning to see the sinewy muscle and tissue underneath—veins that were once red were now earthy brown. His features were nondescript but forming, like an unfinished silicone mask; it was as if someone was moulding his face into existence.

He wasn't going to be here long, and I knew that I would see his face soon.

It happened on the 6th day.

I woke up feeling groggy, hungover almost, and my vision was blurry when I opened my eyes. My first instinct was to look at him, but for some reason, I really didn't want to. I could feel this panic in the deep recesses of my body; like something really bad was about to happen. You know how people feel this sense of impending doom right before a heart attack? That was how it felt. My heart was beating incessantly against my chest, my teeth were chattering, and my palms were clammy. This didn't feel right. *I* didn't feel right. I forced myself to get up and look—I knew that I had to. What I saw made my blood run cold.

I woke up next to a dead body and now he had a face. Oh my god, his face.

I fainted.

When I regained consciousness, I couldn't see—everything was as black as the night sky. I tried to move, and I couldn't—my body felt stiff and heavy. Why couldn't I move? In the distance, I heard a voice, a man's voice—he was speaking.

"Hello? I need the police, please. This is going to sound unbelievable, but I've just woken up and there is a dead body in my bed, and it has no face. Please send someone."

THE SOLITUDE OF IVAN PETROVICH

Loneliness is a silent killer, not something you can easily discern, and often it is unbeatable.

If you're lucky, you may be able to drag yourself from the depths of the depression that constant solitude can cause, but most of the time, you aren't so lucky. I wasn't so lucky, you see.

I haven't any family, any friends and I live alone. I never knew how that happened; it just did. Don't get me wrong, I have acquaintances, who doesn't? But I never considered them real friends, not really. There is a difference between a real friend and an acquaintance—the former will care if you die. So, you see, when I vanished and was presumed missing, no one ever thought to check my apartment—because no one actually knew where I lived. No one cared to know.

But I wasn't missing, I still am not missing. I am very much here, in my apartment and I always have been, and I think, I always will be. It was difficult to come to terms with it to begin with, but eventually, I grew accustomed. You just have to, don't you?

Of late, some neighbours have been complaining of a foul smell that emanated from within my apartment—the smell of rotting eggs is how it was best described. I was sitting in my favourite chair as I so often do, listening to the incessant knocks that plagued my door, but I just couldn't get up, you see.

So eventually, my door was forced open, and that was when they found me.

I was slumped in my favourite chair, you understand. The chair that I never left, the chair that I will never be able to leave. I was somewhat mummified, my body in an advanced stage of decay. My still fleshy right arm lay on the dust covered table, clutching a bottle of vodka. Its contents barren, like me.

Loneliness is a silent killer.

A MOTHER'S GRIEF

A mother's grief is something unimaginable, something fundamentally impossible to fathom unless you have had first-hand experience. It isn't something *I* understood when it happened in my family. To *my* mother. My mother wasn't a fragile woman, it just wasn't in her nature. She was strong-willed, firm and fierce, something that I had always lacked. It wasn't until the death of my brother that I noticed a drastic change in her.

A *terrifying* change.

My brother Michael was always my mother's favourite, he was the apple of her eye. I always came last when it concerned her, a secondary child. One that she probably wouldn't have birthed given a second chance. She never made me feel like that, but deep down, I have always known. Was I jealous? Maybe a little, yeah, but it wasn't like my mother never loved me. She did. Just not as much as she loved Michael.

Michael died when he was just 21 years old—a tragic, gruesome death. *Too young to die*, everyone said. *He had so much to live for.* It was true; he did. His death was macabre—something that you don't hear about every day. It left a mark on us all, but it stained my mother's soul the most.

It knots my stomach thinking about it—about Michael, but I think it's something that must be told, must be shared, and I long to understand why it affected my mother the way it did. Grief touches people differently. I am aware of that, but the way she was acting wasn't normal, it was downright strange.

It was a Wednesday, I think, the day Michael died. The day that my mother's life changed. I don't know the intricate details that surrounded his death, but I was told enough. My mother discovered his body in his one-bedroom flat. She found him hanging from a light fixture in his bedroom, all limp and rigid. His head was hanging on by a thread, lopsided—his mouth was slightly ajar with blood trickling from the sides. The most disturbing thing about it was that he was almost flayed. His flesh was barely attached to his bones. It hung off him like an ill-fitted suit, like it didn't belong to him. We didn't know what could have done something like that, we didn't want to know.

His death was investigated, of course. Police were baffled, naturally. No one could figure out what happened. Some freak accident? A grisly murder? Either they had a dangerous killer on the loose or Michael did that to himself. I was inclined to go with the former. I was scared for a long time, had nightmares daily, thinking that whoever did this would come after me. I feared for my life.

My mother? As I said, she became withdrawn and aloof. She spent weeks, *months,* shut away in her bedroom, only venturing out for necessities. My mother didn't cry. She didn't do anything that you would consider normal, really. I couldn't reach her. No one could.

Things became even stranger when we discovered that Michael's body had gone missing. He'd only been in the ground a few days. The dirt had barely dried before he was plucked from the earth. No one knew why. The police were still preoccupied with finding who or what did that to my brother in the first place, so the fact that his body went missing seemed to drop down their priority list. Life was in turmoil. I lived in constant fear, the terror attached itself to me like some sort of parasite, making a home deep in my heart. I worried for my mother, though, worried what this would do to her. She refused to see me every time I attempted a futile visit and wouldn't answer my calls.

So, one day, I decided to just turn up unannounced. I knew where my mother kept her spare key. I hated to invade her privacy like this, but I was worried sick, terrified, and I needed to make sure that she was okay. That she hadn't met the same grizzly fate that Michael did. I didn't know why I feared that, but I did.

My mother's small house was eerily quiet and dark. When I stepped in, I felt the cold seep into the pores of my skin—it made the hairs on my arms stand on edge. The kitchen and living room were shrouded in darkness but I knew where my mother was, I knew she'd be in her bedroom. Doing whatever it was she had been doing the last few months. I gingerly made my way upstairs, the fear gripping me tighter than ever.

There was a faint light emanating from my mother's bedroom, illuminating the gloomy hallway. It almost looked like candlelight. I stood outside the door for a few minutes, gathering my manic thoughts. I knocked on the door, faintly at first.

"Mum?"

Nothing, no answer.

I knocked again, much louder this time. That was when I heard something stir within. I touched the handle; it cooled my sweaty palm. It was unlocked. I stepped into the room and recoiled at the repugnant sight that greeted me. The smell assaulted my nostrils—it was the smell of rotting flesh mixed in with sweat and stale dirt.

Michael lay in the middle of the floor, surrounded by dripping candles. My mother sat beside him, her hands deep inside his open chest cavity.

"Mum!" I screamed.

"What are you doing?!"

She turned her head and looked at me. Her small, fragile face was lathered in blood, and she smiled, a wide smile that stretched from ear to ear. She removed her hand from inside Michael and in her palm, she held a shrivelled-up heart, and it was *beating*. She lifted it to her parched lips and bit into it. The bright red liquid seeped out of her mouth as she chewed the stretchy flesh. Her eyes were glassy—outright deranged.

"I'm going to bring him back, Sarah."

"He's going to live inside me, and I will give birth to him once more. It will happen. *He* said it will."

***

It's safe to say that I called the police. My mother was declared mentally unstable and committed to an institution. A mental breakdown, they called it. Complete and utter fracture of the psyche. She was a suspect in Michael's murder for a while, but eventually, that was ruled out. They still haven't found who did that to him.

I visit her often, as much as I can really. Recently though, I've discovered something *disturbing* about my mother. Something I can't quite get my head around, in fact, no one else can either.

Yesterday, when I visited her, I saw that she was *pregnant.*

JUST A HUG

"Please, all I want is a hug."

The woman stared at me, her eyes filled with disgust, disdain, and terror. The sight of me repelled her. I knew that much. I'm repugnant; a creature only darkness could accept. I've tried so desperately to come to terms with my ailment, but the older I got, the harder it became.

Do you know how hard it is to crave human contact, and yet never receive it? To yearn for what you can't have. It is truly unbearable. The woe to be human and yet always be on the cusp of society—always shunned, always rejected, and avoided. For the longest time, I wished I was never born. I wished desperately to be back inside my mother's amniotic sack—where there was love and comfort. I wanted to be back where it was *warm*. This world wasn't warm. It had never shown me any kindness.

I killed my mother, you know. The doctors had never heard of my condition before they saw me and saw what I did to her. *Her insides were shredded*, they all said. Can you imagine that? I always have. I had always imagined that the insides of my mother looked like shredded beef.

When she died, I was taken away—hidden and shrouded behind white coats, needles, and scalpels. They cut me open so many times; rummaged around in my insides to find the cause of my ailment. They would put me back together again and the next day, it would happen all over. They never did find out what was wrong with me. Why I was the way I was. But they never wanted to let me out, no. A creature like me—one that society could never understand, could never accept. They knew what that would do to me.

But I escaped. I did.

I have walked amongst them now, for the first time since I was nothing but a blood covered babe. It's been wonderful. Oh, how I have ached for this moment. I have exposed myself to them, taken what I have wanted to take. It hasn't come without its trials, though. I live in fear everyday—the thing I fear most is rejection. It's the one thing I cannot handle, the one thing that could potentially push me over the edge. What if this woman rejects me? What if she goes away, like my mother did? What would I do then? I couldn't help myself, though. It's the only thing in the world that I ever needed and that I ever wanted. My condition prevented me from doing what I wanted most. The doctors always told me that I would never be able to hug anyone, but most importantly they told me I didn't *deserve to*.

But they were wrong.

This woman stood before me, the hate and the filth just radiating off her—I could feel it all, and all I wanted to do was hug her. I knew I could take her pain away and, in turn take my own pain away. This is the only way. *I needed this.* I could feel her fear, as I am sure she could feel mine. I was just as frightened as she was. After all, I had never done anything like this before.

"What are you doing?!" She exclaimed as I walked towards her. She stared wide-eyed at the knives that protruded from my skin. The long, sharp blades that have been the bane of my existence. They bulged out of my flesh, pierced my arms, my torso, and my legs. It's how I was born, you see. It's how my mother died— as I came out of her, the blades that swelled out of my skin cut her open from the inside out.

She screamed as I embraced her—the woman. I was showered in her blood as my blades entered her at all angles.

They pierced her organs.

As I smiled to myself, a wave of terror crept over me, chilling my blood.

What if this is the last hug I will ever have?

THE WOMAN WITH NO SKIN

I heard her before I saw her. The woman with no skin.

I found her tied to a tree in the woods behind my house; all shiny and bloody. Skinned alive, she was. When I approached her, she looked at me with such longing, such pain that I knew I couldn't leave her there. Her battered body hung limply against the rotten bark; she was all muscle and bone. When I touched her, she felt stretchy, like she was made of plasticine. A badly made prop from an 80s horror film. That's how she looked.

"What happened to you? Where did you come from?" I'd ask her.

"I came from within," she'd reply.

I couldn't quite grasp her words, couldn't fathom what she meant, but I longed to help her, yearned to save her. At the time, I didn't know why.

"I want to be let back in," she'd say.

"Let back in where?" I'd ask.

"Inside", she'd reply.

Over the next few months, I nursed her back to health and with each passing day, the more alive she became, the better I felt. I couldn't do anything about her missing flesh, but somehow, I knew that she didn't need it to survive. I knew that this woman was born with no skin. It was how she was created. Despite the rapid recovery, I still felt she was longing for something that I wasn't giving her, but each time I'd ask, all she'd say is that she wanted to be let back in, she wanted to be back where she belonged.

One night, she disappeared. I felt such an unfathomable sadness—like my heart had been ripped out crudely from my chest. I grieved for her, and I didn't know why. Then I heard her weeping again, wailing. I found her tied to a tree behind my house. She was overflowing; black, inky blood poured from each orifice.

She was dying.

"What can I do?" I pleaded with her.

"Let me back in", she replied.

I suddenly realised something; the understanding hit me like a ton of lead. I went back, and I retrieved a knife. I sliced my chest open; the flesh unwrapped with such ease—like a lacy corset. I had no blood. I looked down, and I saw that I was nothing but an empty sack of skin; I had no insides, no centre. I was nothing but a vacant pouch.

I looked up and stared into her eyes. I realised then that they were *my* eyes. My mouth quivered, and I smiled. I unravelled the rest of me, opened myself up fully and I closed my eyes.

"Okay, come back in." I said.

THE RATMAN

Have you ever heard of The Ratman? I first heard of him when I turned 17, that was when my life changed forever. Not for the better, I assure you. I'm 25 years old now and it has taken me 8 years to come to terms with what I experienced and the things I saw. I finally feel like I am ready to talk about it—to put *him* into some sort of words that make sense. If not for anything, then for my own sanity.

I don't know if the legend of The Ratman was born in Lithuania or if he exists in different variations across the continent, but I first encountered him when I moved to a little village called Trakai. It was just the three of us, my dad, my mum and me. We were a family ravaged by poverty—as were many families in Eastern Europe, at least back then. So, when my dad lost his job, we could no longer afford to live in the city.

I absolutely detested it. I loathed the little ramshackle, weather-beaten house we found ourselves in. I abhorred the simplicity of it all. Want to know what I hated most of all, though? It was the *people* that lived there. The superstitions. You know how small communities are. Tight-knit and untrustworthy. I guess in this case, the people of Trakai had their reasons. *The Ratman* was their reason. I understand that now.

I didn't believe any of it, not at first anyway. The first time I heard about The Ratman was when I met Jurgis. I was in Trakai for maybe a month or so when I met him. I didn't really have any friends. I didn't *want* any, but Jurgis drew me to him. Maybe it was because he was a loner, like me.

"Hey, Lukas, you ever heard about The Ratman?" He asked me one day, nonchalantly.

"No? What are you talking about?" I asked.

"The Ratman, Lukas. I am talking about The Ratman." He said, not taking his eyes off me.

"Well, what the fuck is The Ratman?" I asked him, annoyed.

"It's this half man, half rat thing that lives in the woods nearby. He takes little kids, bad little kids. Do you wanna know what he does to them? Boils their heads in a kettle. He slurps out your brains through a straw once your head is nice and cooked." He said this with such a degree of certainty, so matter of fact. Like something he plucked from a textbook. There wasn't a shred of doubt in his voice as he spoke. It was unsettling. His mouth twisted into this detestable smirk that chilled my blood—I didn't like it.

"I'm not interested, Jurgis. So just stop it." I said.

"But he exists, Lukas. We can't deny him."

"Why are you being so weird? Just stop."

I didn't know what had gotten into him. The shift in conversation was so sudden. He stared at me with vacant eyes—they were lifeless and without emotion. He was beginning to frighten me.

"He's going to take someone soon. Watch yourself." He said, his words drilling into my heart. I didn't know what to say. I was rendered mute. Perhaps it was the fear or the unexpected shift in his attitude. I couldn't be certain.

Then he blinked suddenly, and an expression of utter confusion lined his face.

"What were we talking about?"

"You were talking rubbish about something called The Ratman. What the hell, Jurgis?"

"Who's The Ratman?" He asked, his face a picture of puzzlement. Now he was looking at me like I was the crazy one.

"Go screw yourself, Jurgis." I said and went home.

***

When I got home that day, I couldn't shift The Ratman from my thoughts—the idea of him swelled and grew in my mind like a tumour. The curiosity gnawed at me until I could no longer hold off. I had to know more about him. I didn't know why.

As I had mentioned before, we were a poor family, however, my dad kept an old, beaten PC in our living room that he occasionally used to peruse the internet. He never usually let me anywhere near it, but my parents weren't home that evening, so I took the opportunity to use it and see what I could dig up on this Ratman.

The search engine brought up some very thin, elusive results. Most of them being threads on Reddit. I stumbled upon a subreddit called r/loreoftrakai and saw that it was littered with literature about this apparently very real and very abhorrent creature. There were numerous posts made by hundreds of people about their encounters with him, the theories they had about him, that sort of thing. It was classic urban legend lore. Each thread was different, offering independent theories about what the Ratman was, what he looked like and, most importantly, the atrocities he is supposedly responsible for.

There were a few that caught my eye.

u/lurkingintheshadows wrote an extensive, detailed post about what the Ratman looked like. Reading it chilled me.

The Ratman is known to take many forms, that's how he gets close to you but once he has you, he reveals himself. He is tall and skeletal with skin as pale as the moon. So pale that he glistens, as if his stretchy skin had been doused with bleach. Sometimes, his body is covered by dark, filthy fur. His arms protrude from his torso at strange, awkward angles—he always looks like he's coming in for an embrace. He sniffs out your fear with his elongated snout.

His face is the most frightening thing you will ever see. His mouth is twisted, crooked—always smiling, always grinning. The reason he does that is because he knows he has you. It makes him happy, makes him joyous. His eyes bulge from within their sockets, in a perpetual state of surprise—they shine in the moonlight, drawing you to him. He doesn't have any eyelids. Have you ever wondered how someone sleeps without eyelids? The Ratman doesn't sleep.

So watch out, don't let The Ratman fool you. If you do, you'll lose your head.

Don't go into the Pasakas Forest.

My skin tingled, as if a thousand insects had scurried across it. It was downright creepy and there was more, *so much more*. The accounts differed—others wrote that The Ratman had a literal rat for a head, others said he had a man's head but a rat's body. The one thing they all had in common, though, was the fact that they all stated The Ratman had no eyelids. There were various detailed write-ups about what The Ratman does to you—all too horrifying to even recount. The Ratman liked heads, is what I gathered.

The last thing that caught my attention was the latest post, made just a few hours before I found the page. It was a rhyme. It was simple, amateur, but it sent thousands of daggers into my heart. It was written by someone called u/NAMTAR.

If The Ratman comes for you
We'll say a prayer or two
There's nothing you'll be able to do
He doesn't flee to a simple "shoo"
His wrath is fierce, he is a beast
For your head is his to feast

I didn't linger. I turned the computer off and went to bed. My dreams were plagued by images of The Ratman and that god awful rhyme.

The next day, I was tired, groggy, and I had this strange feeling in the pit of my stomach. Like something bad was about to happen—I couldn't shift it. I went to school, seeking out Jurgis. He was the only one I could talk to.

When I got there, I couldn't find Jurgis anywhere. It was unusual for him; he was never late—punctuality was one of his stronger traits. Then I heard all the hushed whispers, saw the huddled groups—it was as if I was observing a herd of penguins in the wild. What were they all talking about? As I walked the hallway, I heard broken murmurs. So many voices talking at once.

"… hasn't been seen since last night."

"… they found so much blood."

"… what could have done something like that?"

It was Jurgis. He was… missing. That's what they all said. I felt sick, impotent with fear. My stomach was in knots, twisting tighter and tighter until I was sure I was going to throw up. The police were apparently not doing anything to help. *"We have to wait 48 hours,"* they said. *"Nothing we can do until then."*

"Sure he will turn up soon." They all said.

But he didn't.

I just knew that something bad had happened to Jurgis, and it had something to do with The Ratman. I don't know how I knew that, but I just did.

I went home. I yearned to get back to that subreddit, hoping to find something, anything, that could give any hint as to what could have happened to Jurgis.

Thankfully my parents were out, they always were. I jumped back onto the computer and found myself on r/loreoftrakai once more. Whilst perusing old posts, I saw that there was something *new*—I scrolled back up and my heart froze when I saw the username. It was *Jurgis.* He had posted a picture of himself in the middle of the woods, his face obscured by darkness. He was *smiling,* but I could see the fear that was hidden in his eyes—it was primal. He had written something above it.

Will you follow me to The Ratman's lair? I see you watching. I'm here, I'm waiting. Will you come?

I don't know why, but it felt like it was directed at me, somehow. I felt compelled to find him, to save him. I had to try, didn't I? He was my only friend in a world full of monsters. That message had to be for me.

Pasakas forest wasn't far—the village of Trakai was small, so it didn't take me long to reach the edge of the woods. The sun was setting and there was something ominous about it—like a scene plucked straight from a horror movie. The trees swayed gently in the evening breeze, alleviating the somewhat suffocating air that I felt settle around me. The sun was blood red, a jewel that hung in the middle of the sky, making its descent. I felt the fear tighten its grasp on my quivering heart. I was paralyzed with fear, but I had to go in.

Pasakas forest wasn't big and there was only one trail. So, I knew where to go. I followed it until I saw tiny specks of blood splattered on the nearby shrubs and on the barks of the trees. I knew I was close.

I slowed my pace, walking tentatively—I was shaking with fright. What was I doing? Before I could answer that question, I saw something in the distance. Something was moving, obscured by the trees in front. I stopped; my heart drummed incessantly in my chest. As I neared, I saw something that appeared to be in the shape of a human being with its head hovering over something that lay on the ground below.

It was a body… or what was left of it. I saw an arm, a foot and a tongue lying strewn a mere few feet away. *What the fuck?* When I looked up, I saw the abhorrent thing that was hovering over the mutilated corpse.

It was him.

I saw his body contorting from a distance, his bare and exposed eyeballs glistened—wet and dripping with sap. They bulged and swelled out of their sockets. *He had no eyelids.* He held something in his hand; it was a straw.

I almost screamed when I saw what was beneath the hand of The Ratman. It was Jurgis's detached head. I couldn't recognise him at first because his features had melted, like they had been boiled. His flesh was charred, dripping like candle wax, and he had no eyes. The top of his skull had been removed, and I almost vomited when I saw that the straw The Ratman held in his hand was nestled *inside.*

He lowered his head and *slurped* Jurgis's brains through the straw. Like he was drinking a milkshake. I saw liquified brain matter trickle out of the sides of the creature's mouth.

I think I finally threw up then. It was disgusting, abhorrent and every other adjective that I could think of that could have summed up that moment. I started crying, backing away. Wanting to be anywhere but there. Then The Ratman lifted his eyes and stared at me. I don't know what happened then, but his face started to *change,* to morph into something else. He changed into Jurgis before my eyes.

"You came." He uttered, a detestable smiling spreading across the face that wasn't his.

I bolted. I ran until I couldn't breathe—ran all the way home. When I got there, drenched in sweat, the sight of me panicked my parents. I couldn't speak, couldn't utter a single word. Police were called—I tried to explain to them, tell them everything, but no one believed me. Hell, they even suspected *I* did something to Jurgis, for a while anyway.

Jurgis never came back, just as I knew he never would. His body was never found either. I think they went to the place in the woods where I saw what I saw, but they found nothing, not a single trace. The Ratman covers his tracks well. I have always remembered that.

A few months later, my parents managed to get back on their feet and we moved back to the city. I went into therapy for a few years. I tried to forget Trakai, I really did. When I turned 20, I moved to London—hoping to forget everything about my life back in Lithuania. I did for a while. Being in a big, busy city really helped me with that. It was refreshing.

Lately though, my mind has been wandering back to Trakai and The Ratman. I knew I was dipping a toe in far too dangerous waters, but I couldn't help myself. One question just lingers and swirls in my mind like cigarette smoke.

How does he sleep with no eyelids?

WOODEN BOX

When I woke up, it was suffocatingly dark. I felt my chest tighten as if an old, shrivelled claw had wound its grip around my lungs and squeezed tight. When my eyes adjusted somewhat, I looked around in a panic; wondering where I was. When I realised, the panic and dread hit me like a ton of bricks.

I was in a splintered wooden box; it seemed to be just the perfect size for me. As if someone had measured it exactly. My feet didn't touch the bottom and my head barely scraped the top; I fit in like a glove.

I didn't know who I was, and my memory was completely blank, like a canvas. I had no memory of anything before waking up in this box—I was a foetus and my amniotic sac was an ambiguous, cold and dreary hunk of wood. I didn't know my name; I didn't know who my mother was, and I felt this overwhelming sadness wash over me, accompanied by an inability to catch my breath.

The air was sparse in here; dry. I knew I had to calm my nerves, or I'd be dead soon. Funny how despite not knowing anything about myself or my life; I still had this overpowering urge to survive. I guess the base primal instincts to fight were much more powerful than we originally thought.

Strangely though, I had this oppressive feeling of familiarity; like I'd been here before, but that couldn't be, could it? It must have been the recycled oxygen messing with my brain. I could hear faint but audible sounds coming from above; rushed voices going at a million miles per hour. I smashed my fists against the top. Fragments of wood pierced my skin, but it was no use. No one could hear me.

Then, as if out of nowhere, I felt something brush my hand. It was a bit of string. I was certain it had not been there previously. I pulled on it and I heard a faint bell; it was slight, but it shattered the silence and rang incessantly in my head. It was followed by a loud bang and the lid opened.

Bright light assaulted my eyes and when they adjusted, I saw so many faces; all masked in white.

"The experiment failed," one of them said.

"We'll have to start again. Wipe him." Said the other.

***

Doctor's notes.

Experiment no. 352 has failed. Subject fails to remember what he has done before his incarceration. The order is to persevere until memory has been recovered. The punishment is for the subject to relive his crime over and over.

Reason for incarceration: Burying his daughter alive.

THE HAG

I have this fixation with maggots. I bet that's not something you hear every day, but here we are. It's not an ordinary obsession and isn't one I've had for very long but the story I am about to relay to you is paramount in understanding this compulsion. Not only am I obsessed with maggots, but I also collect them, and I dissect them—this is all to understand what happened to me.

You see, I *must* understand the reasoning behind my encounter. It's all I live for these days.

My name's Martin, and I am from London. That doesn't matter so much, but I thought it prudent to give some context before I delve into what happened to me. I am 35 years old, and I used to work on the London Underground. Used to is important here because it's imperative that you remember that I no longer work there—I no longer do anything, really. Not after my encounter with The Hag.

My job wasn't glamorous by any means; I was essentially a bin man, collecting rubbish left behind by commuters throughout the day. My job involved a lot of night work. I covered Old Street station; one that doesn't operate throughout the night, so after 11pm, that's when my shift would start. I would go around both the southbound and northbound trains and I would collect all the crap that people had left behind. Londoner's love to litter. It was never anything too exciting; my black bags would be filled mainly by coffee cups, discarded newspapers and food wrappers. Occasionally I'd find something of value like a book or a wallet, but otherwise, nothing of import.

It was a boring job, to tell you the truth, but I wasn't invested. It was just something that pulled cash into my bank account every month so that I could enjoy the finer things in life, like a pint on a Friday night.

Anyway, getting off track here. The reason I'm here, the main plot of this story, happened on one of those mind numbingly boring nights. I normally have music on when I work because I can't stand the eerie silence that permeates throughout the deserted trains that I service. Anyone would get creeped out doing what I did, so yeah, music helped a lot. What I did had become almost ritualistic—I would always start at the front of the train and work my way through to the back. It would take about 2 or 3 hours to traverse both trains.

The first hour of that shift proved to be uneventful; I had only picked up around 3 coffee cups and a scarf that someone had left behind when I saw something out of the corner of my eye; a reflection in one of the windows. It was an old woman. She sat with her head down on one of the seats in the far end of the carriage. Her face was obscured by her hair; hair that fell about in messy clusters about her hunched shoulders and back. At first, I had thought that perhaps she had fallen asleep—this does happen, not very often, mind you, but I *have* seen it.

"Excuse me, miss?" I asked, suddenly confused by the fear that dogged my voice.

She didn't respond but instead, started to sway, ever so slowly from side to side. I'm not going to lie, this freaked me out quite considerably and I started to back away; about to go out and find someone else, anyone else that could help. Suddenly, I didn't want to be there alone.

At that moment, she started to croak. It's hard to describe the noise that escaped from her, but it was throaty; like someone had been scraping her tonsils with a butter knife. I found myself unable to move. Her swaying had fastened in pace; she was throwing herself from side to side. Her grey hair flew wildly in all directions and still, I couldn't see her face.

Then suddenly, she stopped moving.

She cocked her head, as if sensing something. As if sensing *me*. I regained my composure and was just about to run as fast as possible when a pale, white hand shot out of her ragged robe and grabbed me by the wrist. Her grip was *so strong*. I couldn't free myself, no matter how hard I pulled.

"What do you want?" I asked, meekly.

A brief silence passed before I heard that throaty sound again. She seemed to be trying to speak, but no words were coming out; none that I could understand, anyway. Then her hair parted as if touched by the wind and her face was revealed to me.

I recoiled in horror at the sight of her. Her eyes were crudely sewn shut; I could see dried blood where her eyelashes were supposed to be. The tone of her skin was deathly pale with a hue of magenta; like she'd been dug up. Her mouth was open slightly, askew, and as I stared into her horrifying face, she opened it. From within it she spewed maggots the colour of vomit. They dropped and slithered down her chin onto the floor. Even though she didn't have any eyes, I knew she was staring deep into my own.

She looked down, and I did too. The maggots! The writhing and slithering mass of them were forming words. Before I knew it, they had spelled out something that struck terror deep within my heart.

Everything you hold dear will be taken away.

Then quickly, they morphed and spelled out something else.

She starts in 5 days.

I know how this sounds, but it happened. Then she exploded; her blood, guts and viscera covered me and the inside of the train. I was immobilised, unable to move whilst her entrails dripped from the collar of my shirt. It felt like hours had gone by. When I looked up, the interior of the train glistened and gleamed like it had been cleaned. Everything was as it was before.

I quit my job that very same night.

***

A lot of you are probably wondering what it all meant, and I did too, for a while. For days following the encounter, I dreamt of her and the words that her mouth maggots formed.

Everything you hold dear will be taken away.

Then, five days after the incident, my whole world fell apart.

It started with my mother. I was asleep one night when my phone rang—it was my sister. She was hysterical, babbling on about maggots. Apparently, our mother was found dead in her home; her throat had been slashed from ear to ear. Stuffed inside were thousands of squirming maggots.

The police were at a loss; there were no clues. Nothing that led them to my mother's killer, but deep down, I knew who it was. It was The Hag.

I hadn't even had a chance to arrange my mother's funeral before *she* took my sister. Katherine was found with her body carved up from throat to navel. I don't think I have to tell you what was inside. The police dubbed them both the works of a serial killer and worked tirelessly to find out who did it, but I knew they'd never find her.

I was a broken man after that. I had a joint funeral for both my mother and sister; I mourned their loss greatly. The grief I felt was a fathomless pit of despair; one that I knew I'd never crawl out of, but I was determined to do one thing before I ended it all.

I wanted to find The Hag and ask her... why? I knew that evil didn't need a reason to be evil. Evil sometimes just... was.

Finding her again has been my only purpose, and I am determined; one of the only things she was unable to take away from me. I must find her, and I must find her maggots, no matter what it takes. I will avenge my family.

DIGGING

Have you ever felt a profound urge to do something? And if you didn't do it, then it would cause you great pain and immense distress? This exact thing has been happening to me. It was this intense feeling in the pit of my stomach, in the deep recesses of my subconscious. I had to do this *thing* and if I didn't do it, something horrible would happen.

Do you want to know what it was? It's bizarre really and I feel incredibly foolish for even admitting it. Every day, I've been waking up, walking up to my window and staring at this unassuming spot on the grass in my garden; wanting *so* desperately to dig it up. The urge grew stronger with each passing day, and I knew that eventually, I would have to comply. I knew there was something awful underneath that earth, something that I didn't want to find.

It may seem trivial to you and maybe you're thinking that it isn't a big deal. Why not just dig the hole? What's the worst that can happen? Well, sometimes the worst *can* and *does* happen.

This deep, cavernous *yearning* had been gnawing at me, clawing at me like vultures at a corpse and I could feel my hands. hands that were almost not my own, grip the shovel.

Just dig.

So, I started to dig. I dug into the dirt; the coarseness of it hardly bothered me. The sweat from my brow poured in buckets onto my tired hands, but I didn't stop.

The deeper I got, the more overwhelming the feeling became.

Keep on digging.

Dig, dig, dig.

I was digging for days, weeks maybe. I couldn't say. Time was nothing but a vague concept that had become entirely alien to me. I was covered in soot and dried blood caked my hands from gripping the shovel so tightly. The strange thing was, ever since I had started this endeavour into the earth, the sun hadn't come up once. The night was perpetual, everlasting, and cataclysmic.

I wasn't scared though, I just kept on going, digging deeper and deeper. Until I hit something.

Something hard.

I clawed at the black earth, my fingernails splintered; the blood flowed and mixed with the dirt. I couldn't feel the pain though, I was manic; *hungry*. Then I happened to stumble upon something that I didn't expect. Underneath the earth was a small wooden box.

I stared at it for the longest time, the swirling patterns on the wood hypnotised me. I opened it and when I did, I felt the most unimaginable pain; every single nerve ending fired at once. I collapsed into the blood covered dirt, convulsing violently.

The box snapped shut with a violent thud and buried itself back into the earth.

Before I faded, I heard a voice.

"Soul number one thousand and forty-three gathered. Mission complete. Onto the next one."

EERIE WHISPER STREET

When I first moved to Umber Heights, USA, I was struck by how picturesque it was. It felt like it had this hidden history that no one knew about—like a town that had been a witness to something deep and unfathomable. At the same time though, it had this modern and contemporary feel to it—the hum and bustle of a city that I had left behind.

My point is, I liked it. I liked how being there made me feel, and a fresh start was what I desperately needed. I wish I knew then what I know now. If I knew the events that would unfold a few short months later, I would never have moved. I guess hindsight is not a luxury that we are bestowed.

I adjusted to life in Umber Heights swiftly and discovered a certain enthusiasm for walking that I never really had before. I walked *everywhere*. I guess it's easier to do that in a small town, but it's certainly something I fervently enjoyed, and it gave me a whole new outlook on my new home. I'd spend hours of my day traversing new territories and discovering the incredibly intriguing nooks and crannies of Umber Heights.

I guess that's where my story begins. I think it was a Thursday when it happened, a beautiful August summer day. I remember it being an absolute scorcher and I finished work early that day. I couldn't resist another one of my daily strolls through the parks of Umber Heights, so I made my way around slowly, enjoying the sights, the smells and the many sounds of this thriving little town. I came upon **Blackwater Park**. A park that I had frequented on many of my walks over the last few months. It's stupendously large, bigger than any park I had ever seen, and no matter how many hours I spent wandering through it, I had never gotten to the end. That day was going to be the day that I made it all the way through, all the way to the mysterious end. The day was young, and I was determined.

I traipsed through the foliage of Blackwater Park and soon I found myself somewhere that I had never been before. The vegetation and greenery looked different here; it didn't *seem* right. It looked real and vivid, but when I touched it with my hand, it felt rigid—like hard plastic. Confused, I continued and the deeper I got, the stranger everything became. The flowers, the grass, the trees—everything looked fake; like something out of a movie set. It wanted to give you the appearance that everything there was a tangible, living thing but it wasn't. It made me feel uneasy; churned my stomach. There was no smell, no sound. Everything was so eerily still and silent there; all I could hear was my own quivering heartbeat as I walked.

I contemplated turning back when I saw something—a street sign.

Eerie Whisper St.

I stopped dead in my tracks as I heard a silent whistling emanating from the dead, empty road ahead. *Perhaps it's the wind?* I thought. No, it sounded too concentrated, too *purposeful*; as if someone was out there, obscured and with their fingers in their mouth. It gave me the creeps. I looked around but I couldn't see a single living soul, which was unusual for such a pleasant day. There was no one there but me.

My feet shuffled forward, and I continued, walking toward the street. As I got closer, I saw houses; rows upon rows of them. They all *looked* normal. Like your average, run-of-the-mill homes. They looked like they were supposed to. Open, inviting and, more importantly, *lived in*. Deep down, though, I somehow knew that they weren't.

I found myself in the middle of the road on Eerie Whisper Street, looking around aimlessly. I just couldn't comprehend what sort of joke it all was? Because it had to be a joke. I must have accidentally stumbled onto a film set; this couldn't be real. There were a few stores littered around and the funny thing was that they all looked so incredibly dull and ordinary, but they didn't have a single person inside; it was like everyone just got up and decided to disappear. Or maybe they never even existed in the first place. The air was suffocating; it felt like an old, withered hand had suddenly gripped my lungs tight, squeezing the air out. I tried to catch my breath, but I just couldn't. I had decided then I'd had enough—I ran out of there, back the way I came, through Blackwater Park. It seemed like I was running for hours. The plasticky foliage just wouldn't end.

When I had finally made it out, my heart dropped into my shoes when I realised that I was back on Eerie Whisper Street. *Could I have somehow gone in a circle?* I thought to myself. The whistling was getting louder too—I could hear it all around me and amidst it, there were these faint whispers that assaulted my ears. Vague, sinister murmurs that I couldn't make out. They *seemed* like they were for me, I don't know why, but it's how I felt when they reached my ears. Whoever was making them knew that I was there, and they wanted me to know that they knew.

***

I think 14 hours passed and I still couldn't find my way out. I tried countless times and always, somehow, I ended up back on Eerie Whisper Street. The baleful murmurs grew in volume, and they seemed to follow me everywhere—the longer I spent on Eerie Whisper Street, the louder they became. Everything looked the same, nothing ever changed.

Until one day, it did.

I must have spent two full days in that hellhole when I noticed something different. The distinction was slight, but after you spend days observing the same, unchanging shit, you notice. One of the houses in the neighbourhood suddenly started to look brighter—it didn't have the same chalky hue as the rest. It looked like a real fucking house. The whistling and whispering became overwhelming at this point; the closer I got to the house, the more deafening it became. I felt like someone was shoving razor blades in and out of my ears. I thought perhaps I was hallucinating; I hadn't eaten or drunk anything in two days and God knows what that can do to a human body, but I knew it wasn't anything good. I tried to eat the apples from the apple trees and drink from the lakes around the neighbourhood but none of it was real. So, I thought perhaps this was my brain's way of showing me something that couldn't have possibly been there, like a mirage.

I stumbled toward the house, desperately hoping I'd be able to find some real food, some water and a working phone. As I neared, I noticed that the door was ajar, revealing a bleak interior. The lights were off, so I wasn't sure if there was anyone inside. I stood outside the door.

"Hello? Is anyone there? Please, I need some help." I said, almost crying.

There was no answer. All I could hear was that fucking whistling and the hushed whispers.

"Fuck you!" I shouted, to nobody. I think I was losing it.

Suddenly all the noise ceased, the air was as still and as quiet as a nursery. The silence was deathly, ominous, and I felt like someone was watching me. Unseen, phantom eyes burrowing deep into the back of my head.

"Fuck it," I whispered, and I stepped in.

The hallway was shrouded in darkness. It was empty; I couldn't see anything that would give me any indication that a human being lived there. I continued—there were no light switches, so I couldn't make this any less terrifying for myself. I heard whispers again, only this time, they were coming from a certain area in the house—the living room. As much as I didn't want to, I knew I didn't have any other choice. I had to go on.

When I entered the living room, I screamed. In front of a plastic television set, on a plastic sofa sat a family. There was a man, a woman and two children—by their feet lay a shaggy dog. The faces of the family glistened, as if doused in oil. They wore bland, nondescript clothing that looked too big for their bodies. They sat unmoving, perfectly still, as if posing for a picture. I threw up several times and as I tried to leave, they all slowly turned to look at me—their heads moved rigidly, emitting a scraping noise. They were all smiling; a permanent Barbie smile that never left their lips.

"Welcome to our home." They all uttered in unison.

Then they all tried to move; their arms and legs made these odd mechanical motions. They all jerked forward, unsteady on their feet—robotic. I slowly backed away and then I ran. I ran as fast as my weakened legs would take me. I ran back into Blackwater Park, knowing that my attempts to escape were futile, but anything was better than that inhuman family. I looked behind me, but it was so dark that I couldn't see anything. I could still hear them in the distance though, along with the whispers and that unbearable whistling.

I ran headfirst into a tree, and everything went black.

***

When I woke up, I was lying in the middle of the street just outside of Blackwater Park. I must have looked pitiful because there were people gathered all around me, concern and worry lined their faces. I think someone was calling an ambulance, and I was being offered water—which I took willingly. Everyone looked *real,* at least. I sighed with relief.

I was taken to the hospital where I was treated for dehydration; the doctors all put it down to a heavy night. No explanation necessary—no one would have believed me anyway. I was discharged a day later.

I know that everything I saw was real. I know that Eerie Whisper Street was real and that I had witnessed something inhuman that lived there. I had no idea how I found it, and I had no idea how I escaped. I was just glad that I did so that I could tell my story, a story that comes with a warning.

If you ever find yourself in the quaint town of Umber Heights, USA and you stumble across a quiet little neighbourhood named Eerie Whisper Street, I beg you, don't step foot on its treacherous soil. You might never get out.

SCAB

Scabs are one of the most loathsome things, aren't they? They itch and they sting; sometimes leaving distasteful scars on your body. Especially if you peel them off before the cut has had a chance to fully heal. That's one mistake that I made.

I work in construction so acquire random cuts on my hands and arms almost daily. It's something I've grown used to over the years and to be honest, it normally never bothers me. Isn't something I even pay attention to, really. Not at least until a couple of months ago. I woke up one morning to find I had a deep cut on my forearm: long and gaping. Strangely, there was no blood anywhere that I could see, and I was certain it wasn't there the night before. It had already begun to form a scab, but the scab itself was one I'd never seen before.

It was deep brown in colour with sharp, jagged edges: detestable looking and smelt repugnant too. I had thought the cut was infected so naturally; I visited the doctor. My arm was bandaged, I was given some steroid cream, some pills and sent on my way.

It was bandaged up for a few days before I realised that something was seriously wrong. My arm burned and ached—I unravelled the bandaging and was firstly assaulted by the smell of rotting flesh; sour and sickly. My eyes widened when I saw the scab. It had grown considerably in size; almost doubled and was starting to spread. The skin around it was taut and starkly red; the wound was hot to the touch, and it pulsated. It moved and warped as I looked at it, beating like an irregular heartbeat. The longer I stared at it, the more distorted it had become.

With each passing day, the scab spread further and further; almost covering the left half of my body. By the end, I could barely move. This abhorrent dry as a desert, blood filled crust was taking over; it was *alive*. I knew there was only one thing I could do—I had to tear it off; rip it apart to free myself.

I took a knife to the source and carved into it. The crusted flesh flaked and crumbled, like old bread. I then proceeded to peel the scab, it proved to be as easy as peeling a hard-boiled egg. Unimaginable pain shot through my body, and I cried out when I saw my exposed pink, mucousy tissue underneath. After that, the scab *gargled,* like it was choking, and I no longer had control. It ripped my skin apart as easily as soft dough.

I watched, helpless and virtually skinless, as the scab formed into the shape of a human being.

"You should never rip off your scabs," it said.

THEY ARE HERE

It started about a week ago. My commute to work is gruelling and I spend about 90% of it on the London Underground. It's usually ok if I can get a seat, but those are a rare find and sometimes you are left sandwiched in between people like a sardine. It can be unpleasant. It was on one of these trains that I first encountered the Man.

He was clad all in black, face and body mostly obscured. He had this air of dominance about him; like he was important somewhere in the world. Always looking straight ahead; he wasn't glued to his phone like the rest of us. Something about him both intrigued and disturbed me. Maybe it was his almost carefree demeanour or perhaps it was this perpetual confidence that he seemed to ooze. The thing that disturbed me, though, was his smile that spread from cheek to cheek. It was the smile of a deranged lunatic.

I saw him almost daily. Each day, his smile seemed to widen, growing—spreading from ear to ear. It seemed to happen when he caught the eye of an unsuspecting passenger. They would shift uncomfortably in their seats; desperately trying to get away from his blank gaze. I was the only one that seemed to notice the looks of sheer terror that plagued their faces when he looked at them and I was the only one that seemed to notice when the next day; one man became two.

I know how it sounds. Believe me, I do. But it's true. The very next day, I found myself staring at the same man... twice. I sat, utterly stupefied, thinking myself gone mad. Both men were identical to the blemish. It seemed no one was safe from the men in black.

Things only got worse. The next day, I found myself looking at the same man…four times. They were multiplying, and still I was the only one that had noticed. Something was happening here. The vacant expressions of these horrifying men burrowed deep into my soul and their unhinged smiles invoked this primal fear in me.

Who were they? What did they want?

***

I looked out of my window this morning and my heart beat against my chest like an incessant drum. Everyone had been replaced—as far as my eye could see. The street was littered with these strange, terrifying men in black.

I watched as they walked, their gait so unnatural and stilted—like they weren't used to it. Their faces were blank, vacant. Not a shred of humanity lined their plastic features.

They consume us. I've seen how they do it. Their bodies twist and morph—their chests unfold, and we are absorbed. I don't know why, and I don't know how, but they are here. They are here for us.

I think I'm the only one left and they'll be coming for me soon.

Please, is there anyone else out there?

MY BROTHER JOHN

Every night when the clock struck 12, I watched my brother die.

It didn't matter where I was or what I was doing—he'd be there without fail. He would simply stand and stare at me, his hollow eyes and gaunt face expressionless. I had to witness his demise over and over. Even in death, I couldn't escape that bastard.

I'd always hated John. We were twins, you see, and ever since we were both, he had it out for me. Even as we lay in my mother's womb, sandwiched in her amniotic sac—he would absorb all the nutrients—robbing me of my development. The bastard was evil, no doubt. I know the whole evil twin thing is cliche, but he wanted me dead. I just knew it.

As we grew older, John really declined. Even though we were twins, I was better than him in every single way, and he hated me even more for it. The animosity he carried for me lit up his eyes like two little candles; they burned red each time he looked at me. Maybe that's why he did what he did; the envy ate him up from the inside. He tried to kill me so many times. It started off small at first, but then it escalated to a terrifying degree. My parents couldn't take it, so they sent him away.

Before John left, he told me that one day he *was* going to kill me and that I was destined to die by his hand.

"Only one of us can live," he hissed at me.

I will admit, his words affected me; etched deep into my soul, marking me like a branding iron. But as time went on, I slowly forgot about him. Before I knew it, 20 years had gone by, and John was nothing but a faded stain on a frayed carpet.

A few months ago, John died. Heroin overdose, they said. He was found slumped in a chair in his flat; covered in his own shit and vomit. A needle hung limply from his mauve arm; his veins protruding, oozing crimson. He was skin and bone, they said, unrecognisable.

I started seeing him soon after that.

He'd never say a word; just slip the needle into his arm and push gently. Then I'd watch him choke on his own vomit, I'd see his throat slowly seize up. His eyes would widen as he succumbed and death creeped in.

Every night, it was the same. Except one night.

When he came, something changed. I could feel myself waning; an overwhelming weakness suddenly plagued my body. John smiled. I watched as my skin turned sallow as my body shrivelled. John retrieved a needle from his pocket and slowly walked over to me. He didn't say a word; just slipped the needle into my arm and pushed gently.

I watched as John became alive.

My throat convulsed, and I was choking. For the first time, John spoke.

"I told you Jason, only one of us could live."

THE THING GROWING INSIDE

Doctor Garcia: Mary, let's talk about what happened.

Mary Williams: Do we have to, Doctor?

Doctor Garcia: I'm afraid that we do, Mary. It's been a few weeks and the police need a statement.

Mary Williams: I don't know where to begin, Doctor Garcia.

Doctor Garcia: Just begin at the beginning, Mary. Take your time.

Mary Williams: Well, I don't exactly know when it started. You know? I don't know when the thing got inside of me. I guess I first started to notice it when the hunger came.

Doctor Garcia: The hunger?

Mary Williams: Have you ever felt true hunger, Doctor Garcia? The sort of hunger that grips you from the depths of your soul and doesn't let up? It was like that. I was famished all the time. Just about ready to devour anything and everything put in front of me. I noticed something was wrong when I ate the rotting corpse of a rat that I found in my basement. The sinewy, chagrin innerds of that rat tasted amazing, though.

Doctor Garcia: You ate a...rat?

Mary Williams: Yes, doctor. I ate a fucking rat. Things only got worse from there. I barely recognised myself anymore, but now I know it was that detestable thing.

Doctor Garcia: What did you think it was, Mary?

Mary Williams: It was a worm, a parasitic organism whose only intent and purpose was to devour me from the inside out. It grew so big, Doctor.

Doctor Garcia: Why did you think you had a worm growing inside of you?

Mary Williams: Because I could feel it, Doctor. It moved so freely in the interior of my body, slithering and gliding within my flesh. I could feel it leaving a trail of slime on my muscles, my bones because sometimes when I touched myself, my skin would feel wet, dampened. It was fucking disgusting. I had to do something.

Doctor Garcia: What did you do, Mary?

Mary Williams: I decided to cut it out. There was no other way.

Doctor Garcia: Tell me about that day.

Mary Williams: I starved it that day. It retaliated, of course. The pain I felt was inconceivable. Like someone was scraping my bones with a dull blade. I took a pen knife and I sliced myself open until my stomach resembled a grotesque smile. I put my hand inside and I fished it out.

Doctor Garcia: Please continue.

Mary Williams: I pulled out the cord of veiny, mucousy tissue and I sliced until it was no longer attached to me. The thing screeched. I looked down at its small frame and I saw its little teeth chatter. Its eyes were barely open, just two little slits full of blood. Its coppery skin was so taut and leathery, like that of an old, frayed book. I took it to the bathroom, and I fucking drowned it.

Doctor Garcia: Mary…

Mary Williams: I had to, Doctor!

Doctor Garcia: Mary... there was never a worm. You were pregnant.

BEAUTIFUL

I've never been beautiful. In school, I was always told that I had a face *"only a mother could love"*. They'd all pity me— *"brains but no beauty"* they'd say. But as I grew older, that all changed. I guess puberty had other plans for me. Everyone was so shocked, even my own mother and father. No one could believe that the ugly duckling had blossomed into a swan.

But I never believed it. I could never *see* it, you understand. All I saw was a grotesque specimen, a face so disgusting and misshapen. A face that deserved to be hidden away from society. Each time I'd glance in the mirror, I failed to see what everyone else saw. All I perceived were my own shortcomings, my own inadequacies. I convinced myself that I had a face that not even a mother *could* love.

If I didn't love myself, how could I expect anyone else to?

Things only got worse after I started seeing *her*. She was the most beautiful thing I had ever seen; a face so defined and deli-cate—like that of a porcelain doll. Her hair fell about her elegant shoulders like a picturesque waterfall. She was everything that I wasn't, and she made sure I knew that *every single day.*

I'd see her every morning and every night, in the mirror.

"You're ugly", she'd tell me.

"You're worthless," she'd sneer.

And with each passing day, I believed her more and more. She had wormed her way into my mind; had burrowed herself deep inside my subconscious with her barrage of hate and loathing. One night, she began telling me to stab myself in the face; she told me I had to fix what was broken. She told me that was my only way out; my salvation was the edge of a knife.

"Don't you want to be beautiful?" She'd ask.

"Don't you want to be loved?" Her eyes would sparkle like two bright diamonds as she'd present the knife to me.

"Yes," I said.

"Then you know what you have to do."

I nodded as I caressed the blade; the cool steel chilled my fingers as I felt the tears warm my cheeks. I lifted the knife to my face, and I sliced; I carved until all I could see was blood. My vision was crimson, but I could still see her beautiful face and she was smiling. I smiled back as I pushed the knife deeper into my flesh; the sound of wet meat filled my ears.

The knife fell, clattering on the floor. I looked up and marvelled at my face; I had done it. It was perfect; like an ice sculpture whose imperfections had been chiselled away. I touched my moistened cheeks; the blood stuck to my fingers as I caressed the nerve endings and the pink fleshy tendrils. I smiled and closed my eyes. I was finally... perfect.

All I ever wanted was to be beautiful, and now I was.

THE PAPER CUT

I woke up one morning with this horrendous stinging pain on the palm of my left hand. Upon investigation, I saw that it was a small paper cut. I won't say that it was painful because it wasn't—it was just uncomfortable; to start with, that is. I paid it no mind at first, forgot about it to be honest with you, but as the days wore on, it really started to gnaw at me. It throbbed, burned, and it started to feel hot to the touch. It almost felt like someone was rooting around on the inside of my palm, scratching and slicing with a jagged piece of glass.

So, I did what any normal person would do, and I put a plaster over it; hoping that eventually it would just go away. It didn't though, and over the coming days, it just got worse and worse. My entire hand felt like it had been set on fire; I could literally *feel* the skin sizzling and melting away, but when I'd look, my hand would be perfectly fine. Obviously, this wasn't normal.

Feeling a little foolish, I went to see a doctor; hoping that I would just be told that my paper cut was infected. Although, the origin of the paper cut itself was a complete and utter mystery to me. I had no idea where it came from. As I sat in the waiting room, my legs jittering uncontrollably; I realised just how nervous I was. I couldn't understand why. When I went into the doctor's consulting room and presented my inconsequential injury; the doctor grinned ever so slightly. I knew what he was thinking—that I was wasting his precious doctor time. But fuck him, I had thought. I was frightened and in pain.

"Now, let's see what we've got here", he said. Speaking to me like a child.

He unravelled my crude plastering and bandaging; when he looked at my paper cut, his eyes widened, and he went as pale and white as a sheet of paper. He leaned in closer and whimpered. His eyes filled with crimson tears, overflowing and spilling onto my lap. I shifted in my seat uncomfortably.

"Err, is everything ok, Doctor?" I asked.

"Y-yes. Perfectly fine. It's beautiful. What's in there." He said, slowly getting up from his seat. He shuffled over to his table and lifted a scalpel. With a quivering hand, he stared into my eyes and began slicing his throat; all his sinewy tissue, his blood-red muscle, was unveiled. It all hung and adorned his neck like a red ruby necklace.

I fell to my knees, tears flowing. I lifted my throbbing hand and looked at the small slit. It swirled and moved like an illusion; I looked inside. Among the red-hot muscle and the tight flesh, I saw a pair of eyes. Then a soft voice spoke.

"Let me out."

I gripped the scalpel and lifted it to my throat.

NEW BEGINNINGS

I've been responsible for a lot of deaths—some call it genocide, but I call it reducing the population; there just isn't enough space here for all of you. Unlike many other serial killers, I don't have a 'type' nor do I have a clear cut motive. The people I kill are random, but they *are* also calculated; I must think carefully when choosing my victims.

I get around too; all over the world, to be precise; there is nowhere I haven't been. My killing methods vary too; sometimes I like to use water, sometimes I like fire; other times I like to use some lethal concoction that I create. I'm very talented, you understand—not to mention highly *creative*.

What you must know about me is that I'm not *evil,* not in the normal sense of the word—what I do is for the good of the planet. You people have been careless, abusive, and I am tired of it. I have watched you destroy this beautiful rock with your technological advancements, with your deadly fume machines, and trust me when I say that she can't take anymore. I have watched you kill indiscriminately; you burn the innocent alive. At least when I do it, it's within reason. I do it because I must, because you have left me no choice. I have been a witness to so much torment. I hear the incessant screams of your children, of *my* children, and I can bear it no longer.

You are all so full of hate, so full of contempt for yourselves and for others. Perhaps it's the undeniable intelligence that makes you question everything; that makes you *so* frightened of your own mortality, so you lash out, take it out on those that don't deserve it. Humankind has always lacked that little thing called morality, and actions have consequences, don't they? They certainly do now.

You thought you could get away with it, but I guess you didn't know that I'd be watching, and I *have* been watching. Every step of the way. There is only one thing left to do. I think this planet needs a fresh start—a new beginning, so I'm planning something, something *big* and monumental. A plan has been growing and brewing within me like a silent, malignant tumour and I am about ready to begin.

Remember, I am doing this for the greater good; the earth must heal—*I* must heal. I am a Mother you understand, I am *your* Mother and I do love my children, but sometimes a Mother has to do the unthinkable. I believe you call it *mercy* and I promise you; I will be merciful.

Even after you're all gone, I'll always be around; creating and destroying. Mother nature always finds a way.

PEEL

I've had this problem for as long I can remember, ever since I was nothing but a new-born babe, all pink and sweltering. *You came out screaming.* My ma used to tell me. I didn't know it back then, but there was something wrong with me. As I got older, I started to realise. I remember the dismal stares, the pitiful looks; the disgust radiated off them when they looked at me, the people I mean. Even my own mother.

I've never been happy in my own skin, and I think that's why—I was born with something rare, something unheard of in the medical world. They didn't even have a name for it, you see. *Just a rare skin condition, there is nothing we can do.* Their words would reverberate in my head, crashing into my thoughts like a wave. It was something I was going to have to deal with.

I guess I should probably get to the part where I explain the problem. I find it hard to talk about it and you'll understand why. It's extremely unpleasant, I can assure you of that. Abhorrent, if you will. Looking at me was like burping and accidentally throwing up in your mouth; the acidity of your stomach contents burned the back of your throat and you grimaced. You know what I'm talking about, don't you?

This condition was… genetic, apparently. Something I inherited from someone in my family—either my mum or my dad, or perhaps it ran deeper than that. It was impossible to distinguish.

My skin was adorned by thick, bulbous blisters that would ooze pus and blood perpetually, leaving a sticky trail of pale pink. Eventually, it would rot; the skin cells would die, wane, and fall off. The flesh would glisten and shine as it slithered off my muscles like a worn, wet plaster. I'd watch my exposed meat swell and pulsate as the blood filtered through my veins. I used to have to get constant skin grafts.

After a while, I couldn't stand it anymore, so I began picking at my skin before it withered. I would finger the swollen holes, dig my fingers into the soft, sinewy flesh, and then pull. It was like picking the meat off a tender chicken bone. It became an obsession, a compulsion; I yearned for new skin constantly. I *needed* it. None of them understood what it was like—to ache for something so viciously. I was willing to do anything.

I have always wondered what it felt like to peel off flesh that wasn't my own. Flesh that wasn't diseased, putrid and dying. This skin that is as smooth as silk, does it peel off as effortlessly as layers of an onion? I caress the velvety surface and I sense the warmth through my rotten fingertips. As I slice the knife through the tenderness, there is one final thing I want to know.

Does it hurt, mother?

TONGUE-TIED

I open my eyes, but I can't see anything, it's so dark. I can feel beads of sweat forming on my brow and that's when I realise that my head is covered by a dusty black sack. My memory is hazy—I can't remember anything from last night. I don't know where I am, and I start to feel the panic bubble up inside; as if a cord has woven itself around my intestines. Getting tighter and tighter with each passing minute. I try to open my mouth to speak, to scream, but no sound escapes—as if I have been made mute. Why can't I remember anything?

I hear footsteps in the distance, approaching slowly. A strong, firm hand grips the sack and rips it off quickly, crudely, along with some of my hair. I think I cry out in pain, but I can't be sure because I can't hear my own voice. My eyes adjust quickly, and I look around—my mind trying to find something, anything, to indicate where I am. I am in a small, barren room; a single light bulb hangs from the grimy ceiling illuminating the splintered wooden chair I am bound to. My eyes turn to look for my kidnapper, but all I see is a hand, a phantom hand belonging to nobody. The hand is gloved and soiled, covered in splatters of a sunburnt brown and a dark scarlet. Is that blood?

The next thing I know, I'm faced with the barrel of a gun, all black plastic and squared edges. It's so close to my face that I can almost see the serial number. I try to speak again, but my efforts prove to be futile. What is going on? Why am I here? *Why can't I talk?* I look ahead, trying to find a face that *must* belong to this terrifying fucking hand, but I can't.

I hear a voice. A deep, booming voice that echoes across the room, bouncing off the walls. It seems to be coming from all sides, it has no source.

"5"

"4"

Why the fuck is it counting down?

"3"

"2"

Oh god, someone help me.

"1"

BANG.

The bullet enters my cheek; I can feel my mouth overflowing with blood. It travels down my throat and suddenly, I am choking. I think I cough, and I am bathed in crimson. I look down, but my eyes are misty, as if covered in film. In the distance, the gun cocks again and the voice speaks. It counts. I try to look up, but the blood is gushing from the corners of my mouth like a chocolate fountain. Is this what death feels like?

BANG.

***

I open my eyes, but I can't see anything, it's so dark. I can feel beads of sweat forming on my brow and that's when I realise that my head is covered by a dusty black sack…

MY TWIN SISTER

Let me start this off by saying that I'm a twin. Growing up, people would always comment on how freaked out they were by Jacqueline and me, how odd it was. *"Isn't it weird how alike you two are?"* People would say. *"It's almost unnatural."* Kids are ruthless, everyone knows that. I was never sure if their lack of tact was down to their undeveloped brains or just plain old cruelty. I didn't think there was anything weird about being a twin, but then I wouldn't, would I?

It never bothered me. I had always assumed that it never bothered Jaqueline either, but that was a mistake that I had learned too late. I took her lack of communication for granted, I had assumed when I should have scrutinised, I was wilfully blind to her transformation when I should have seen. I didn't *see*.

Jacqueline and I were extremely close as children, just like twin sisters are supposed to be. We did everything together, it was almost routine. Anything she did, I did, and vice versa. We were in our own little world that nobody could penetrate, not even our parents—we had this everlasting, unimaginable bond that no one could comprehend. No matter how hard they tried. I knew that it was unbreakable on the surface, but I even went as far as to liken our sistership as indestructible.

at an atomic level and nothing could keep us apart.

After a while, though, things started to change. We were approaching adulthood, reaching that age where we were desperate to be individuals, or I think Jacqueline was at least. I was happy for things to stay the same, I was so content in my own bubble of monotony that I had failed to see how rapidly Jacqueline was changing. It started off small, the changes. They do at first, don't they? That's why you don't always notice them.

I remember being somewhat taken aback when she'd come home one evening.

"What have you done?" I said, eyes wide.

"It's just hair, Jodie." She replied.

I laughed it off, but deep down, it hurt me. I couldn't understand it—why would she want to look different to me? I didn't push it, though. *Hair is hair.* I thought. We were still the same in every other sense and looks were superficial. At least that's what I tried to tell myself. *Looks were superficial.*

Then she started to change her clothes.

She did everything she could to avoid wearing anything even closely similar to me. We would always plan our outfits and everything we owned was the same, but I started seeing clothes on her that I had never seen before. Ripped tights, loose fitting dresses and jumpers—things that didn't look *right* on her, but she wore them anyway. Everything she wore was the colour of oatmeal—bland and tasteless and I couldn't understand it.

I knew something wasn't right, but I just couldn't say anything without sounding deranged, controlling, even. Jacqueline was allowed to wear whatever she wanted—I didn't own her. I tried not to question her, I tried to let her be. I figured she was going through something that she couldn't speak about—something she couldn't share with anyone, even me. I tried not to let the worries and anxieties get to me, even though I could feel them in the pit of my stomach—threatening to overflow and drown me. I was desperate to know what was happening to my sister.

As time went on, things started to get stranger. I could barely recognise Jacqueline anymore. It was difficult to comprehend the utterly insane changes that I was witnessing with my own eyes, but reality can be skewed when everything you thought you knew comes into question. I found myself looking at her and seeing someone completely different, and I couldn't understand how that could be possible.

Our parents were none the wiser. They just thought she was going through 'puberty'. Even when things started to become... terrifying, they chose not to see it—they chose ignorance.

Jacqueline would spend her days roaming the streets of London—I had no idea where she was going or what she was doing. She would come home in the early hours of the morning and would spend the rest of the night creeping around the house. I didn't know what she was doing, and I don't think I wanted to know. Some nights, I would hear her skulking around like a lizard and stop outside my room and just stand there for what seemed like hours.

I'll admit it, I was terrified of her.

The day that I decided to confront Jacqueline was the day I lost her forever.

I remember that evening like it happened yesterday—trauma does that, right? You relive those moments over and over and it doesn't matter how much time passes, because it always stays with you. Time is supposed to be the healer of all things, but I think that expression exists and acts only as a placebo—something you are supposed to tell yourself in the hope that your life could be bearable again. But when something happens that alters your entire existence, it can never be quite the same, can it? No matter what you do.

It was midnight and by this time, I would already be in my room with the door locked. I knew I had to see her for myself, talk to her, see if there was anything I could do to save her from whatever *this* was.

The house was as still and as silent as a nursery—I could hear my own heart drumming against my chest. I had decided to wait in the dark—my only source of light was the night sky illuminated by the moonlight. I didn't want to startle Jacqueline when she returned, so I kept the lights off. I didn't have to wait long before I heard the keys jangle and the lock turn. She was home.

When she stepped into the moonlight, I gasped.

The flesh on her body hung and sagged off her like an ill-fitted suit, baggy and shapeless. The colour of her skin was pale and grey, bruised almost. Her cheeks were sunken in like potholes, her mouth was torn, bloody and cracked—the skin peeled off as she moved her mouth, falling onto the floor like flakes of dandruff. She looked like she was... decomposing. There was no other word I could use to describe it.

"What's happening to you?" I asked.

She opened her mouth to speak, but no sound escaped her chapped lips. Instead, she made the most guttural sound I had ever heard. It was earthy, low and intense—like a growl of someone who has had their mouth sewn shut for decades.

"J-j-odie." It was like she exhaled my name. I could barely hear it.

"Jacqueline, please. Talk to me. What happened?" I pleaded.

She began to move, and I could hear her bones creak and groan like rusty gates swinging shut. The way she moved was so *unnatural*, stunted almost—like watching something in slow motion. She was coming towards me, her hands outstretched. The flesh on her hands was peeling and blistered, red raw like the flesh of a newborn. She limped towards me and I found myself recoiling back at the gruesome sight of her. Even though she was Jacqueline; she was my sister. I couldn't bear to look at her.

"They did this to me." She managed to whisper.

"Who did?" I asked.

"They said shedding old, inferior flesh would make room for new, superior flesh." She croaked.

"What does that mean, Jacqueline?" I asked her. I could feel the tears trickling down my cheek.

She held something in the palm of her hand—it looked like a pendant from where I was standing, but I couldn't quite make it out.

"They promised me I would be different. They promised me that I would be elevated." She said, her eyes lit up like candles when she uttered those words.

"Who are they, Jacqueline?" I asked, taking a step forward. The pendant glowed in her hand, it *radiated* this bright, red hue that almost lit up the room.

"They're going to come for you, too. Just as they did me. They're going to come for all of us." She said, the flesh on her palms drooped like pieces of old kebab meat on a skewer, barely hanging on to the sinewy muscle and bone.

She then began to *shed*. That's the only way that I could describe it. The flesh that encased her bones began to fall away like wet parchment paper, piece by piece until she was nothing but a wet, glistening and sticky skeleton.

"You'll see, Jodie." She spoke again.

I watched as she disintegrated in front of my eyes, melting away like wax on a burning candle, leaving only a small bloody puddle.

That was the last time that I saw my sister.

***

It's difficult to describe the weeks that followed—everything was a blur. Everyone in my little world believed that Jacqueline ran away. She was reported missing, but no one really took it seriously, not even my parents. Police, doctors, family—everyone around me thought it was nothing but a 'phase'. I couldn't fathom how utterly nonchalant everyone was—even if Jacqueline did just go missing. There was no *urgency,* and I couldn't understand it.

As time went on, she was forgotten entirely. No traces of her remained. No one remembered that Jacqueline ever existed. I soon found memories of her slipping from my mind, too. I began forgetting the little things to begin with, like the shape of her face, what colour her eyes used to be, and the sound of her voice. Could that be possible?

The day that I found the pendant was the day that my life ended. I woke up gripping it tightly in my hand one morning, having no idea how it got there. That was the first time I noticed it too, the skin on my hands—it looked thin and pale, almost translucent. They reminded me of my grandmother's hands; aged, faded, and covered in liver spots. What was happening to me?

The changes were slow but evident. After a few weeks, I could barely recognise myself in the mirror. My hair had thinned and fallen out completely; a few wayward tufts remained, but they were wispy and sparse. My skin had become grey, transparent, and flaky. I was putrefying but I couldn't understand why. Something about it *felt* familiar, but I couldn't quite place my finger on it—it was like a long-lost memory.

The longer I held the pendant, the more I aged. But the curious thing was, I couldn't let it go. As much as I tried to release my grasp on the detestable thing, I just couldn't.

When I examined the pendant, the less I remembered where I had seen it before. Have I ever seen it? It was covered in these curious patterns I could scarcely describe and words I didn't understand. It was unlike any alphabet or language I had ever seen but it was what was engraved in the middle that terrified me. It had two heads, supported by an elongated neck. The heads themselves were oddly shaped and lumpy protruding at odd angles. They looked soft, swollen, and filled with fluid. I don't know how I could tell, but I just could. It had no eyes, only barren cavernous holes where eyes should be, and the only thing that covered that bulbous face was an abhorrent smile. It stretched from ear to ear, like it had been carved so that it could be as wide as it was. It was jagged and uneven, much like the rest of it. The mouth was filled with rows upon rows of razor-sharp teeth that oozed a thick, sticky substance that resembled sewage water.

I knew it didn't have eyes, but I could feel it looking at me.

"What do you want?" I asked, barely recognising the croaky whisper that escaped my lips. Hasn't this already happened before? Did it already happen to me, or was it someone else? I couldn't remember. I tried to grasp at the memories like drowning kittens gasping for air, but they slipped further and further from my clutch the harder I tried.

"Shed your skin. Become one with us." It said, extending a sinewy, leathery hand.

"Make room for new, superior flesh, Jodie."

"You promise?" I heard myself asking. What was I saying? Why was I saying these things?

"We promise. You aren't the first and you won't be the last, Jodie. We promise to make your world ours, just like we have with others."

I could feel myself fading, and then everything went black.

"We will give you a glimpse of what it will look like. Close your eyes, Jodie."

When I opened my eyes, my vision was blurry, and I could barely move. When I looked down at my body, I saw that my flesh was charred, blackened, and broken. I was on my back, but I couldn't see what I was lying on—it didn't feel like I was supported by anything but merely suspended in the air. I turned my head, and that's when I saw her. She was fused to me—her skin melted into mine. Who was she? She reminded me of someone that I knew long ago but no longer recognized. For a moment, I thought she looked like me.

I looked around, the sky was black, impenetrable and never ending but somehow I could see. It didn't take me long to see the others. They were all hanging in the air, the same as me—their skin scorched and torn, blended and melted to the one lying next to them. There were thousands of them, all lined up as far as the eye could see.

Then I heard the voice again.

"This is your new world."

MIRROR, MIRROR

Have you ever found yourself staring at your own reflection in the mirror for just a little too long? When you look at yourself for longer than you're supposed to, that's when you start to notice…the little things. Small changes in your appearance—things you've never noticed before.

I started trying it out not too long ago, experimenting if you will and I became kind of obsessed. I'll admit that. My house became a kind of 'hall of mirrors' attraction. Weird, I know, but everyone has a hobby, don't they?

I'd sit for hours just staring at myself in the mirror. Every so often, I'd get up, and I'd go try a different one—just to see the little changes. Surprisingly, there were many. The thing is, though, it was never anything *too* scary or *too* unsettling, you know? At least not till about a week ago.

I was sitting in front of the mirror in my living room, behind me another tall mirror stood, looming. I liked to see the reflections within the reflections—it was more intriguing that way. Seeing not only the differences in my own face but the variances in my surroundings, too. Then, out of nowhere, I could have sworn that my face *shifted*, it fucking moved. I sat perfectly still, expressionless, and I saw the side of my mouth quiver. Almost forming a smile. I scrambled to my feet and, to my horror, my *reflection* continued to sit, unmoving—staring at me with its hollow eyes. Then the mirror me opened his mouth, but he didn't speak, he wailed in a raspy and stunted manner.

Things only continued to intensify over the coming days. I would catch glimpses of the mirror me in my periphery, standing in various dark corners of my house. Eventually, it became a daily occurrence. This shadow of myself materialised just out of my direct line of vision, but he would always, always vanish when I looked straight at whatever mirror he was appearing in. It seemed just *too* unreal at first and for the longest time, I believed that I must have been hallucinating because what other explanation was there? But deep down, I knew that it was real and that somehow, he wouldn't remain a mere shadow forever.

One night, I was dreaming, but something pulled me from my deep slumber—a presence in the room. When I opened my eyes, I immediately knew that something was wrong, *very wrong*. Everything around me was reversed, it was all backwards—mirrored. I looked up, and that was when I saw him. He stood in front of the mirror, facing me, and then he smiled. I could feel my muscles twitching, *morphing* into a smile. He lifted his hand and waved at me, slowly. Before I knew it, the muscles in my own hand flexed and quivered.

I waved back.

THE LITTLE GIRL WITH NO TONGUE

Have you ever heard of that really famous kids TV show *The Saga of The Little Girl with No Tongue*? No? Well, I haven't either. I am positive that it doesn't exist and that it never has. Nevertheless, made up or not; this show changed my life.

I used to spend most of my days lounging on the sofa watching TV, and yes, I am very aware of how that makes me sound. If you're imagining a vast, blubbering slug, then you'd be right. I lay on my sofa so much that most nights, I am certain that I have somehow fused with the stitching. I am the sofa as much as the sofa is me. Is that some sort of esoteric proverb? If it wasn't, it is now. You get the idea, I'm a lazy layabout.

I'd usually fall asleep on the sofa watching Netflix and it was on one of those nights that I first encountered 'The Saga of The Little Girl with No Tongue'. I remember waking up with an absolutely rank taste in my mouth; like I'd swallowed the turd of a horse. My mind muddled and foggy. I opened my eyes, and that was when I saw the vivid writing on my TV screen.

Are you still watching *The Saga of The Little Girl With No Tongue?*

What the fuck? I thought to myself. I was adamant I fell asleep watching 'Trailer Park Boys', so what was this shit? I was curious, though, and the title drew me in. Maybe this was some sort of straight to TV fail? Perhaps it was a hidden gem? Either way, I pressed **yes** and episode 1 flooded my screen.

A single chair stood in the middle of a dimly lit room; the chair seemed to be the focal point of the episode. This went on for a few minutes and I contemplated turning this weird shit off, but then I heard a scraping sound, like someone was dragging themselves along a splintered floor. Moments later, a little girl came into view. Shards of glass protruded out of her waxen skin. A soiled rag hung around her frail, broken body with her hair, wet and greasy, hanging limply on her bloodied back.

"What the fuck?", I whispered in horror.

The little girl got up, albeit with some effort, and stood in front of the chair. I could see her face emerge from within the mess of hair; it felt like she was looking right at me. The silence that filled the room was fucking deafening, and I felt the hair on my skin rise and prickle.

Then I heard a hushed voice, a low whispering that emanated from the TV but at the same time seemed to be echoing around the whole room. It was all garbled though, completely unintelligible, but I could have sworn I saw the little girl's mouth move. She lifted her bone thin hand and pointed at the camera, but it felt like she was pointing at me. Her mouth opened, so fucking wide; wider than any mouth I've ever seen. I thought for a moment that I was looking into a deep, never-ending cave. Her charred eyes enlarged and then suddenly, the screen cut to black.

"Michael, what are you doing?"

You know that phrase—jumping out of your skin? Well, I can attest that it's possible because that's what happened to me. I looked up and saw the exasperated, albeit concerned, face of my girlfriend, Annie.

"I fell asleep, I think. Sorry. What are you doing up?" I asked, sort of not wanting to talk about what I just saw.

"Looking for you, dickhead." She smirked, walking over.

"What were you watching? Don't tell me, was it porn? Is that why you're being all weird?"

I looked up at her, but the joke went over my head completely, I couldn't concentrate.

"Some creepy show, never heard of it." I said. I hated how my voice quivered when I spoke, the fear exposed.

Annie frowned. "Michael, are you okay?"

"I-I'm not sure, I think so. That was just fucking weird." I chuckled, trying to lighten the mood. "Here, I'll show you."

I grabbed the remote, attempting to steady my hand in the process. I flicked Netflix back on, but to my astonishment, the show wasn't there. I couldn't find it anywhere in my 'continue watching' and according to the streaming service, the last thing I watched was 'Trailer Park Boys'. *The fuck?* I thought, panic surging through me.

"Michael, stop fucking around. I'm going back to bed."

"No, Annie. I swear to fucking God it was there. I fucking watched it." I said, the fear and confusion on the verge of overtaking me completely.

I stayed up for hours just scouring Netflix until I just couldn't keep my eyes open anymore—I never found the show.

***

I spent the next few days thinking about the show. That little girl swirled in my mind like smoke, suffocating my thoughts. I felt withdrawn, aloof, and confused as shit. Annie couldn't understand what was wrong with me. She kept prodding and probing, trying to find out why I'd suddenly changed. I tried to explain again about the show, but she just kept shrugging me off; thinking I was being a lunatic.

I found nothing on Google. Apparently, *The Saga of the Little Girl With No Tongue* wasn't a thing. No one had ever made it, and why the fuck would they? It was abhorrent. I started to think that perhaps I'd dreamt it, had some lucid nightmare, but something about that felt stupid; it felt all too real that night.

I decided to sleep on the sofa from then on, in the hope that I would find the show again. I just wanted to know that I wasn't going mental. Annie wasn't happy about it, of course. We argued, and she called me all the names under the sun, but I just *needed* to know. It was becoming an obsession of sorts. It was a little too late when I realised that it was something I should have just put from my mind, buried it deep like I buried my kitten Colleen when I was a kid.

***

I slept on the sofa for 6 days before anything happened—I don't know what triggered it, but something in the room didn't feel right. I opened my eyes and the first thing I saw was Annie. She sat in front of the TV, utterly transfixed by the images that plagued the screen; they flashed and bounced but there was nothing to see.

"Annie, what are you looking at?" My voice sounded alien to me, it wasn't mine.

"Can't you see her, Michael?" Annie's voice was far away, distant.

I looked at the screen. All I could see were these spiraling pictures that made no sense. After a few moments, I thought I saw a shape. A shape of a little girl, the one that had no tongue. I blinked and a microsecond later, I saw the same threadbare wooden chair in the middle of a darkened room. Only this time, the chair was occupied.

Suddenly, Annie started sobbing. She wept and howled like she'd just gotten the worst possible news of her life. I shot up from the sofa and rushed to her side. I looked into her face and her eyes were glued to the TV screen. She wasn't blinking, her little eyeballs were completely immobile. I shook her.

"Annie! Annie! Snap the fuck out of it." I shouted. I screamed into her face, but my efforts were futile.

"She's speaking to me, Michael. Oh my god." She covered her ears and started screaming, but she just wouldn't take her eyes off the screen.

"Annie, please snap out of it." I think I started crying.

I tried to unplug the TV, but to my dismay, the image persisted. The little girl with no tongue continued to grind away at my girlfriend's sanity, at *my* sanity. After what felt like hours, the TV finally switched off. Annie's facial expression changed. It warped like clay mold and she was herself again. She looked up at me, her eyes filled with pain and confusion.

"Michael, can we go to bed, please?" It was such a peculiar thing to ask, but I was so exhausted that I didn't feel like I had the power to protest.

***

I woke up a mere few hours later and noticed that Annie wasn't next to me. I looked around in the darkness and saw a faint white glow emanating from our living room. My blood solidified in my veins and my heart turned to stone as I made my way to the room. As I neared, I heard voices, hushed whispers.

"You want me to come inside?"

"How long will I have to stay?"

"Okay."

I walked in and I saw Annie with half her body submerged inside the television. I was frozen to the spot; my body was rigid, and I couldn't move. I screamed for Annie to stop, to come back to me. By the time I was able to move my stiff bones, Annie was fully inside.

I stumbled and ran to the TV, but I was too late. I saw Annie, and I saw *her* walking away, hand in hand. The little girl with no tongue turned to look back at me and she fucking *smiled*. A detestable, loathsome smile that made me sick to my stomach. The TV switched off but before it did, I saw the thing that was pretending to be a little girl inserting long, singed and rotted nails into my girlfriends' eyes.

***

I tried to find Annie, I tried to find the show, but it never came back, and Annie never came back. I didn't give up though, I bought multiple TV's, and I watched them day and night. In hope. I steal a few hours of sleep a night just to keep myself going. I have made it my life's mission to go into whatever fucked up place Annie was taken into. I have made it my life's mission to find that fucking thing and to kill it. Burn it, stab it; anything.

No matter how long it takes. I will find *The Saga of the Little Girl With No Tongue.*

SCREW YOU WORM

Have you ever seen a water flea? They are these minuscule, translucent spiny creatures—imagine a baby with a twisted, broken spinal cord and a bulging stomach and you'll understand. These adorable little organisms can only be seen through a microscope, and they dwell in acrid swamps and filth infested lakes. The reason I know this is because I collect them.

It's not a job or anything. I'm no scientist. It's simply something that I have a great fascination with, a fondness, if you will. My habit is not limited to just crustaceans—I get worms too. Horsehair worms look like strands of long hair in the water, dark in colour, like your own hair in a plug hole. They twist and writhe. We have flatworms, a truly unique invertebrate, soft bodied. Their heads look like pins.

You get the idea. I collect parasites.

Recently, I discovered a parasite that I had never encountered before. The Primary Screwworm. And let me tell you, it is one evil, detestable bastard. It is a worm that will literally screw you from the inside out, leaving you a mess of rotting flesh, scar tissue and deep, putrefying wounds. It thrives off the body of a warm-blooded mammal, it *feeds* off the muscle tissue, picking it apart like a well-cooked chicken bone.

I have seen what this thing can do to cattle. The process is swift, agonising, and death occurs within a matter of days. It is inconceivable. I can only imagine what it can do to a human being.

I have another hobby, you see. It's currently tied up, laying in its own vomit in my basement. The process has already begun. The Primary Screwworm larvae is easily ingested through water and a

bone-dry human body deprived of fluid will drink literally anything.

It begins in the intestines; they start off looking like flea bites
and quickly turn into open, oozing galvanised wire cuts. These
little maggots multiply once they get inside and within a day or so,
they make their way through the kidneys, the heart, the lungs; just
devouring organ after organ. The party really kicks off when they
get to the brain, though. Once they get there, it's over. They attack
the neural tissue, rendering the host virtually a vegetable. Next
comes the spinal cord, instant paralysis. The pain neurons in the
brain are still active and they fire away at the nervous system
endlessly like lightning bolts. A very painful, torturous death
occurs.

I have a day job, a crappy cashier's gig in a generic supermar-
ket—not something I'm invested in. I think I know how to make it
interesting though, I know how I can make it *exciting*. I think it's
about time that I released the *screw you worm*.

UNDER THE SEA

"When did we last hear from them?" I asked my fellow colleague.

"It was sometime yesterday. They went down and didn't come back up." He responded.

"And they picked us for the rescue mission, huh?" I joked.

"There was no one else." He said, scowling.

"Okay, how far have we got to go?"

We flew across the desolate land, a land that has been ravaged by fire long ago. A planet scourged by disease, by war. The inhabitants destroyed, ravaged; the savagery of their conflict is painfully apparent.

"We're nearly there now. Their last known location."

We approached the vastness of the water. A deep blue sea greeted us as we neared, an ocean that has been a witness to unimaginable bloodshed. I could still see the specs of blood scattered across the calm sea. We hovered above.

"How far deep do we have to go?" I asked.

"We lost contact about 28,000 feet in, but it goes deeper." He said.

"In we go then." I smiled.

We breached the sea with our vessel as we descended; the light of the smoke covered sky quickly fading. There was no sun here anymore and darkness came over us swiftly. Our vessel lights were our only guiding grace, our only light. As we reached the ocean floor, our eyes were assaulted by mountains and mountains of corpses; their bodies ravaged by the elements. They were unrecognisable as a species that they once were. Still, we had further to go.

"How much further until the location?" I asked my colleague.

"Not far now. We are almost there." He said, his eyes scanning the darkness.

We came upon the vessel of our friends. It stood abandoned on the ocean floor; it was eerie. We knew one of us would have to go out there and thankfully, my colleague volunteered. Our small vessel halted, and our eager eyes surveyed the area. We couldn't see anything, so we thought it was safe to come out. Before he exited, I grabbed his arm.

"Remember where we are." I said.

"I know. I'll be careful." He said, tightening his grip on my hand.

I watched as he exited the craft. He waved at me as he floated toward the boat of our missing friends. I watched in horror as the decayed corpses of those that inhabited this planet came towards him. Their bloated bodies surrounded him; their loose skin floating in the water, still attached. Their eyes bulged as they grabbed at him, pulling at his appendages with incredible ease. They grabbed at his tail, his many eyes, and they devoured him.

I had no choice, I had to leave him. I flew off the desolate rock as fast as I could—the third planet from the sun loomed behind me.

Rescue Mission Report

Four of our comrades were lost on the planet they used to call Earth. The homo sapiens have evolved beyond what was expected, turning into savages. Any hope of recovery is now lost.

BROKEN MEMORIES

I suffer from severe insomnia—so much so that I sometimes must be sedated in order to rest properly. They say that you can survive 11 days of no sleep consecutively and the longest I've ever gone is 9 days. The doctors thought it was something psychological, something that I apparently didn't want to face, but how could I face something I didn't know existed? I've been to countless therapists, participated in thousands of sleep studies, and nothing helped. I started to believe I was a lost cause and that I couldn't be fixed. They told me it was trauma I suffered growing up—that was the only possible explanation and I'd blocked it out to save myself from a nervous breakdown.

I wasn't always like this, you know. At least I don't think I was. I couldn't always trust my memory though—I didn't recall much about my childhood, but I guess who does, right? I had no recollection of anything before I turned 16 though, which I realised wasn't normal. Subconsciously, I was aware that something happened to me. I just didn't quite know what.

That was before.

Recently a lot of my memories have been coming back to me though—my brain was like the lost and found. I didn't know what belonged to me, but I rummaged through, nonetheless. Hoping to discover a little bit more about myself, rediscover who I was before the insomnia. Get back some of that identity I was clearly missing—a little piece of myself I lost. I was like a puzzle with missing pieces, and I was desperate to find them so that I could put myself together—be a whole person instead of just a half.

It started with these little fragmented flashes of memory. They would invade my head. Crash into my thoughts like unrelenting waves of a stormy ocean. It was small things I'd remember to begin with—like what I got for Christmas when I was 11 years old. Which was a Monopoly board game, by the way. Then other, more significant memories would flood in. I started to remember my old childhood home—the one I used to live in with my grandparents.

I knew that I didn't always live in London. I knew I was from somewhere else. My parents made sure to remind me of things like that, things they knew I didn't remember. Like I was originally born and bred in Lithuania, a little small town called Vilnius, and that I lived there up until I was 16. After that was when I started to have trouble sleeping and began losing my memories.

It was the way my parents talked about our life back then. Their eyes would glimmer like stars on a warm summer night. As if whatever went on there was a secret—something they themselves wished to forget. I never probed, never asked. Perhaps it was that part of me that knew that those memories were the reasons behind my ailments as an adult.

But soon, I had no choice but to remember.

We lived in a more rural part of Vilnius, filled with picturesque forests. I remember now how it felt living there—it was like living in a postcard. It was that beautiful. My grandmother was one of those Eastern European traditional women—a true Babushka. The sight of her used to warm my insides like hot milk. I started to remember things like that—these little feelings that being there used to invoke within me. I remember it being like a drug, the countryside and all its quietness. It's nothing like living in a busy city—where everything is so unbelievably *loud.*

I'm going a little off track here, aren't I. These memories were just so utterly new to me, so alien that I can't help reminiscing about every small detail. Anyway, growing up, my grandparents used to live in this huge apartment block—it would traverse the clouds, almost. We lived on floor 11. I guess now that I was much older it didn't seem as high. But as a kid, it seemed humongous. Frighteningly so.

I remember I used to love exploring all the floors—take the lift up and down. It was a silly little game I played as a lonely little girl with no one to call my friend. I'd start on the 1st floor and work my way all the way up to the top—the building was made up of 15 floors. It used to take me a while exploring each one. The lift used to take forever. But eventually, I'd get to the 15th floor and feel like I'd just got to the summit of Mount Everest. I was so proud of myself every time. My grandma used to call me her little explorer. It stopped being a game as I grew older though, instead it became almost ritualistic—something I did daily. Old habits die hard, I guess.

I think the traumatic event happened when I was 14 years old.

I don't remember the day, but I remember that it was noon. I was about to play my game when I noticed something different when I stepped into the lift. There was something above floor 15— a new button. It looked old and worn, like it had been pressed too many times. Above it, in faded letters, read **No.16.** I frowned. There was no 16th floor, I knew that. I'd been up and down in this lift and traversed this building countless times over the years— there had never been a button for floor 16. This building only had 15 floors; I knew that. So, what in the world was this?

I was curious though, so I pressed it—wouldn't you? I guess kids are just inquisitive that way. Seeking out things they shouldn't, and I should never have sought out floor 16. Considering what it did to me.

As soon as I pressed it, I felt the lift roar with life. It groaned and rumbled quietly, like distant thunder, and then it slowly began to move. The journey up felt much longer than it usually did. I found that my nerves were quite wrought. I was anxious, and I didn't know why. I watched each button light up as the lift made its way up—when it finally got to floor 15, the lift trudged along ever so slowly. Eventually, it stopped.

The doors opened and the first thing I saw was...nothing. The corridor was shrouded in complete and utter darkness—an eerie silence endured and felt like it lasted forever. I wasn't scared at this point, not yet. I wasn't afraid of the dark. I took a step forward and immediately noted the drastic change in temperature—it felt below freezing in there. I shivered as I continued, my body shaking uncontrollably, going almost rigid from the cold. Then suddenly, the corridor flooded with light. It was so bright I had to shield my eyes. I stood with my eyes shut for a while, almost too scared to open them. When I did, though, the thing that I saw in front of me was almost too grotesque to put into words.

Before me, leaning against a charred, blood covered wall, stood a large wooden cross. It was the biggest cross I'd ever seen in my life—jet black in colour. It was adorned in blood red carnations, which were woven through it, covering it from top to bottom. I looked down and saw dozens of other flowers laid out haphazardly—there were lilies, roses and orchids. All the colour of crimson. My eyes widened in horror as I saw what was in the middle. It was a doll. Its still plastic face unnerved me, its eyes seemed to follow me as I moved around the cross. Its lips were parted, slightly ajar and blood stained. It wore ragged, torn clothes that I thought were supposed to be a dress.

In the middle of the doll's chest was a knife—plunged deep into the middle. As I leaned in to look closer, I saw that it, too, was covered in blood.

I somehow managed to tear my eyes away from the ghastly sight in front of me and I looked around. There were two flats on either side—both looked too old-fashioned to be a part of the building. Everything looked burned to a crisp—bloody and raw. It was as I stared into the door on the right that I saw it was glowing. It looked like it was on fire. Then something stirred within—a shape. I stood so still, not daring to move a muscle for the fear that I would be heard.

The silence was absolute, until it wasn't. Amidst all the terror that surrounded me, I heard a cry—the wail of a small child. Its harrowing cries grew louder and louder and before I knew it, the whole corridor shook with the sound. It was deafening.

I tried to leave but found that the lift was gone and there was no button to call it back. I was stuck.

Tears rolled down my face as I frantically tried to find a way out. Then, out of the corner of my eye, I saw the glowing door open. From within came a roaring fire. It licked the edges of the door—the smoke swirled and rippled. Out of the mouth of the fire came a man. When he stepped into view, I recoiled at the sight of him. His skin was scorched to the bone, completely blackened by fire. His clothes were melted into his flesh; now a part of him. I saw exposed muscle and bone; all charred. It was still *sizzling.*

The smell was unimaginable. I know most people say that burning flesh smells like bacon. Well, it doesn't, the smell is more akin to beef that's been left burning in a pan. It's the *fat* that smells like bacon. Mixed in was the horrifically sharp smell of sulphur. I remember vomiting. I was so dizzy.

Despite my bleary vision, I saw something in the burned man's left hand. He was dragging something, a body. Its small frame was awash with flame, but I could see it stirring, trying to wriggle out of the burned man's grasp. *It was a child.* A little girl, to be precise—she looked just like the doll that was embedded in the cross. To the detail. Even to the bloodied mouth. She was crying, screaming, but the burned man paid her no mind. Then I heard her say something that chilled me to the bone.

"Please, daddy. Stop!"

He stopped then and looked down at her meek frame

"I told you what would happen if you did that again. Now you'll have to answer to God."

"I didn't do anything. Daddy, please. You're hurting me."

As they both got closer, I saw that she wasn't so little. She was a lot older than I had first thought—a teenager, maybe, a young woman.

He dragged her to the cross—which was now bare. The carnations, the flowers and the doll were all gone.

"I will drive this evil from you." He hissed; smoke escaped through his teeth as he spoke.

He suspended her in the middle of the cross; held her by the throat. I saw his eyes, and they glowed, so bright, but there was no kindness there. No love. He hated this girl, and he yearned to harm her; I could feel it. In his other hand, he held a knife—it was sacrificial. One of those with strange symbols etched into the blade.

I don't know what came over me, but I couldn't let this happen. As unexplainable as it all was, I couldn't let him kill her. I ran over and screamed. I shouted at him. He stopped, slowly lowered the knife, and turned his gaze toward me.

His face changed, it warped—his charred features rippled right in front of my eyes. Then he spoke to me.

"I curse you." He said.

"May you never again rest and may flame, death and misery forever haunt you until you die."

Then, without hesitation, he whipped around and stabbed the girl in the chest—plunged the knife so deep into her heart.

"Daddy…" she whimpered, blood flowing out of her mouth.

He walked back toward the flame covered door, walked inside and shut it behind him. I ran over to the girl, but she was nothing but a plastic doll again.

The lift had reappeared again, and I ran as fast as I could to it. I was hysterical, beside myself. When I got back, my grandparents were frantic. Apparently, I had been gone for 5 hours. Was that possible? Could it have been? I didn't know what was real anymore.

***

My grandparents thought someone attacked me at first, even after I tried to tell them what I had seen, what I'd experienced on the 16th floor. They told me that the 16th floor burned down. It hadn't existed for a long time. Apparently, it burned down 30 years ago—burned down by a man that had lost his mind.

This man had murdered his wife and his daughter and then set fire to their bodies—himself included. No one knew why. It was a tragedy. It was not long after that I started having trouble sleeping and losing my memory—it was his curse.

I still can't sleep, but now I know why, and it hasn't cured me. It hasn't given me back that part of myself that I so desperately needed. If anything, I suffer more now. When I do rest, my dreams are plagued by those horrific memories of that man's burned face and the anguished cries of that girl. Confronting those memories hasn't helped me heal. I realise now that perhaps some memories should stay forgotten. They should stay buried, locked away, and never be allowed to resurface again.

I used to yearn for sleep and now all I want to do is stay awake because every time I close my eyes, all I see is fire.

THE SUN

"Daddy, why can't we see the Sun?" I asked my Father.

"Because no one would understand you, my sweet." He replied.

"Daddy…" I whispered.

"Yes, my sweet."

"Why am I different?" I asked, tears filling my eyes.

"You're not *different*, you're just special. That's what you are, Aviary, my darling." He replied, gently stroking my cheek.

There were three of us—Savant, Cora and me, plus our Father and Mother. Our parents had long protected us from the dangers of the outside and have kept us sheltered. Why, you ask? I've never known. I guess it's because Savant, Cora and I are different; I don't know how, but it's what Father always tells us. Father always says we were a beautiful miracle, born from a fragmented star—I've always found comfort in that.

Father and Mother keep us in a special chamber, deep below their house. They say no one can ever find out that we are here because if they do, we'll be taken far away and we'll get hurt. I often hear Father talk about men in white coats. I've never seen them, and I know that I don't want to, so I keep quiet; I try and overcome my desires to see the outside world—to see the Sun.

One night we were asleep, Savant, Cora and me and that's when we heard them. Father burst in and he dragged Savant away by her hair. Cora tried to stop Father, but he hit her so hard that it broke one of her legs, snapped it as if it was nothing more than a thread-bare twig. As I tried to mend the fractured bone, the muscle, and sinewy tissue—I pleaded with Father. Why was he hurting us? What had we done?

"I can't let them find you", he uttered through gritted teeth.

Cora and I were left alone in the darkness and all I could see were Cora's terror-filled eyes, shining and glistening in the dead of the night. We couldn't understand. Father always said he loved us.

Then we heard loud bangs, and that was when the men came—men clad all in black. In their hands, they held machines that made our ears bleed. They killed Father and Mother, left their bodies riddled with holes that oozed and dribbled with blood. Before Father died, he spoke.

"I tried to keep the world safe from them."

When the men saw our charred, bulbous bodies, they recoiled in horror. They took us away then and took us to the men with the white coats, who prodded, poked and pierced us.

They should have left us well enough alone, though. When we mutilated the men in black and the men in white, we went outside, and we finally saw the Sun. The Sun warmed our faces as we shrieked; it reflected off our many teeth, and we smiled before we swallowed it whole.

THE LIFE OF A TORSO CHILD

My parents were pretty charitable, always wanting to make a difference. Always wanting to *fix* everything and everyone. So, when they brought my adoptive brother home, I understood completely, and I didn't complain. Despite his disturbing appearance. He sort of made you recoil and do a double take when you looked at him. *No one wanted him,* they would say, and to be honest, I wasn't surprised.

They said he was found on the streets like that, and no one knew what happened to him or why he looked the way he did. It was truly grotesque, but after a while, you got used to it. If anything, I felt tremendous pity. Abhorrence mixed with pity, you could say. *That poor bastard,* I'd sit and think as I stared at his dismal frame. What was left of it, that is.

You see, my new brother was nothing but a torso. He had no arms; he had no legs, and his mouth was *sewn* shut. Have you ever heard anything more sickening, anything more detestable than a little boy who was nothing but a torso? I can't say that I have. His stumps were adorned by deep, thick scar tissue. They looked like they had been cauterised. I found it hard to bond with him. How do you bond with someone who doesn't have a mouth?

The poor bastard had to be fed through a tube. I didn't even want to know how he pissed or how he shat. The thought made me shudder. A thick, putrid lump of bile would rise in my throat as I watched my parents try and give him *some* sort of quality of life. The strange thing was, though, when I'd catch him looking at me, his eyes would be vacant, devoid of all emotion. I guess it was understandable.

One night, I woke up to a peculiar sound, a kind of awkward smacking of lips. It was coming from my brother's room. I never liked being around him alone, so I rushed to get my parents, but when I went into their room, I found their bed empty. I made my way to my brother's room, albeit slowly. Admittedly, I was scared. As I neared, I heard a wet slurping, the sound someone makes when they're finishing a milkshake.

When I opened the door, I found my brother squirming and writhing through an endless pool of blood and shit. I saw the corpses of my parents, their innards crudely ripped out by a set of razor-sharp teeth. The face of my brother was manic, deranged—the sutures that lined his mouth were ripped off awkwardly. I couldn't comprehend how. He looked up as he saw me, a wide smile spread across his bloodied face. When he spoke, his voice was so guttural. Completely unlike the voice of a child.

"I can be whole again." he said.

PLASTIC FACES

"Patrick, for fuck's sake, are you really this drunk again?!" Diego's voice sounded far away, muffled, as if submerged under water. I opened my eyes and my vision immediately blurred. I looked up at Diego and I saw double; his skin swelled and morphed as I looked at him. If I didn't know better, I'd think he was made of plasticine. I reached my hand out to touch him, to *feel* his skin under my moist fingertips. I wanted to know if he was real.

He hit my hand away. The pain was sharp, instant and undeniable and it brought me back to reality somewhat.

"Dude, what the fuck?" I managed to stammer. My head felt a little clearer, less foggy, and I fumbled around for my phone. That was when I realised, I was on the floor. I didn't know how I got there. The last memory I could grasp was being at Diego's flat for his leaving party. I remember drinking the vodka red bulls, drowning my lungs in them. Then the memories danced in my mind, forever out of reach. I don't remember much after the 12th drink, except for waking up with Diego's crinkled face looking down at me. He looked mad.

The blackouts were becoming more frequent, severe. The guilt rose in my stomach; I could feel the acidity travelling up my sternum, but then again, it was probably the alcohol. *What did I do this time?* I wondered to myself. The shame threatened to engulf my body in its cold, dispassionate grasp. The familiar feeling of dread swirled and swished in my stomach; I wasn't sure whether I wanted to vomit or not, but I could feel the bile rising in the back of my throat.

"I'm done with you, Patrick. I tried so hard to be sympathetic to you, to hold on to that feeling because of what you've been through, but I can't excuse this constant shitty behaviour any-more." He said. I could hear the gall in his voice.

"How you behaved tonight was unforgivable."

"Shit man. What did I do?" I croaked. My voice sounded raspy; like I'd been screaming all night at a concert.

"Let me guess, you don't remember, huh?" Diego said, rolling his eyes.

In that moment, I fucking hated him.

"You know I don't." I said, the irritation apparent in my voice. My body ached and throbbed, like I'd been hit by a cement truck and maybe I had been, who knew. I couldn't remember shit. Before I could stop myself, the dreaded words just rolled out of my mouth—the words I knew that Diego didn't want to hear. The words that *nobody* ever wants to hear from someone like me.

"I'm sorry."

"Fuck you." He said and walked off. His words cut deep, and I winced, but what did I expect. There is only so much a person can take and, in his case, Diego had been taking a ton of shit from me ever since Michelle.

Michelle was my sister, and she's been missing for 3 years. It was my fault entirely, there isn't a doubt in my mind about that. I don't remember much about that night; my mind is a blank canvas every time I dare to try and grasp those miserable moments. The memories are sporadic, distant, and blurry. I remember being in a bar with Michelle and a couple of other friends from work. I remember *feeling* happy, elated—like nothing could touch me. I remember Michelle crying, shouting and telling me how much she hated it when I drank that much. I remember feeling anger, sorrow, and denial. I remember staggering to the underground, getting the night tube—I was sure Michelle was there with me. Then the memories are too scattered; a puzzle I struggled to piece together.

I think I passed out on the tube; I did that a lot back then and when I woke up, Michelle was nowhere to be found, vanished—it was as if she was swallowed up by the earth itself. There was an extensive search, overzealous news coverage, and naturally, I was under suspicion. When the CCTV footage was reviewed, though, I was quickly ruled out when they saw me pass out with Michelle next to me and then wake up, alone. Everyone was at a loss—there was no sign of her.

I knew it was my fault, though. The guilt had been eating away at me like a cancer; just savaging my organs, stripping away at everything that made me human. Metaphorical necrosis, that's what I called it. I should have been there, watching out for her—I was her brother, and I should have protected her. I didn't though, and I fucked up. Something awful happened to her. I knew it; could feel it in the very fibre of my being.

The heavy drinking didn't stop there. You'd think that after something so utterly inconceivable, the trauma of it would break the cycle for me, but it didn't. If anything, the overwhelming grief made me want to drink *more*, and that's exactly what I did.

After Diego's outburst, I knew that I would never see him again, but somehow, I didn't care. *What's one more burnt bridge?* I thought to myself. There are only so many times a person can hear the word 'sorry' before it begins to turn their stomach, before it becomes meaningless, before they can no longer bring themselves to ever forgive you. With Diego, that time was then.

I picked myself up off the floor and looked around—it was late. The night was mild and balmy; I could feel the sweat from my brow leaking into my parched mouth. I licked it absentmindedly and the salt stung my arid tongue. I checked my watch—it was 11.44pm. I still had time to catch the last tube home. I stumbled towards Old Street station, which was my usual haunt—I knew the twists and turns of the station by heart.

The putrid, hot air pummelled me as I entered—it was like stepping off a plane somewhere tropical. I suddenly felt so tired, my legs wobbled like jelly, and I struggled to carry my own heavy body. I felt like I had bags of lead attached to each limb. I walked in a daze, completely unaware of my surroundings. Thankfully, the station was empty, which didn't surprise me since it was a Wednesday; not many people drank their lives away on a Wednesday night.

When I got to the platform, I noticed how eerily silent it was, the normal hustle and bustle of rush hour entirely absent. I glanced at the schedule and the last train was arriving in 2 minutes—I felt relief, the night was nearly over. I was desperate for sleep. I looked around and saw that there was no one else there but me; that felt wrong somehow. It made me feel uneasy. I desperately wished to see another human face. I couldn't fathom why.

It wasn't long before I heard it, the unmistakable sound of the approaching train; the scraping, singing metal was deafening. The screeching sound of the wheels grated my ear drums; my head felt like it was being stabbed repeatedly with a blunt knife. As the train approached, I found myself frowning—it looked... curious. Most of the tubes nowadays were rusted over and covered in filth, but I'd never seen one quite like this before. It was historic—something you'd see in a museum. The decaying paint was the colour of oatmeal and flaked in odd patterns; like someone had attempted to scrape the colour off with a pen knife. The windows were oddly shaped too, not your run of the mill long rectangular design. They were small, oval, and tinted.

As the train pulled up, I saw my own confused face staring back at me. I looked utterly deranged, eyes wide and bloodshot. I felt my breathing quicken, I was nervous, and I didn't know why. I didn't want to get on the train, but I felt I didn't have a choice—it was either that or I slept on the streets and that would have been an entirely new low for me.

The train doors creaked open, and I gingerly stepped on. The doors shut briskly behind me as I did so. I found myself sweating profusely; I couldn't tell whether it was this alien anxiety I was feeling or the alcohol excreting out of my pores.

I looked around and something immediately struck me; there was no fucking smell. Usually, the underground always had a scent. You always got a whiff of something recognizable when you stepped on. Whether it was the sickly scent of perspiration, stale dampness or the unmistakable, faint aroma of vomit—there was always *something* there. Something undoubtedly human. But there was nothing there that night and it fucking terrified me.

I tried not to think about how uncomfortable I was and sat down, hoping for the journey to go as swiftly as possible so I could get the fuck off. But I couldn't help but feel like I didn't belong, like I shouldn't be there, and I couldn't pinpoint why. The bright fluorescent lights of the train hurt my eyes, formulating a raging headache. I closed them for just a moment and before I knew it—I fell asleep.

***

It was the sudden jerking motion of the train stopping that woke me. For a moment, I forgot where I was and when it dawned on me, I panicked. *Shit, did I miss my stop?* I thought to myself and looked around. My eyes were still blurry, and everything danced and swirled in front of me; I rubbed my eyes, willing them to adjust. When my vision cleared, what I saw nearly made me pass out.

Throughout the entirety of the carriage, on each individual chair, sat a mannequin. Their plastic skin glistened in the luminous light; looking slick and sweaty, like they'd been doused in gasoline. Their bodies were bereft of clothing, and their rigid limbs were positioned at odd, twisted angles. I felt my chest tighten, my heart was going a million miles per hour, and it felt like it was going to kick my chest open. I stood, unable to move—my flesh felt cold, clammy, and entirely not like my own. My legs managed to move a little, and I stumbled backwards, trying to put as much space between me and those pale, plastic monstrosities.

I moved swiftly toward the doors in an attempt to pry them open, but my efforts proved to be futile when they just wouldn't budge. They were sealed shut. I hit the emergency button and still, nothing happened. I rushed to the windows but everything outside was jet black, impenetrable. I fumbled the ledges of the windows, looking for an opening, but there wasn't one. There seemed to be no way out.

I turned back around and immediately wished I hadn't.

The mannequins were all facing me. I realised then that I didn't notice their faces at first and I desperately wished that it stayed that way because their faces... oh my god. They were the most grotesque things I had ever seen. Something that I knew would be imprinted in my mind forever; like branding a cow. Their faces were... human. The flesh that hugged their faces was bloody, loose-fitting—like a badly matched suit that didn't quite fit. It didn't belong to them, it wasn't *theirs*. The mouths were small, thin slits adorned by dry, crimson coloured saliva. They didn't have any eyes—just blank, gaping holes where eyes should have been. But I could *feel* their gaze and it terrified me.

"What do you want from me?" I shouted; my voice was gravelly; like I'd swallowed sand.

That was when their human masks began moving, *morphing* into a horrifying smile that spread from ear to ear. The dry blood that caked their faces cracked and flaked, falling to the floor. Then one of them stood up. The movements were odd, jerky and mechanical—I could hear its artificial limbs scraping and moaning. That's when I saw the sign. I didn't know how I didn't notice it before. It hung limply on the mannequin's neck. The crudely written words sent daggers through my heart.

NAME—*Constance Brourard.*

REASON—*Pageant mum. Forced own child to participate in harsh contests in a quest to alleviate her own failures. Selfish. Vain.*

DURATION—*7 years and counting.*

I found myself struggling to breathe. My chest was so tight, as if grasped by a frosty mechanical hand. This had to be some sort of sick joke. It couldn't be real. Nothing like this could ever be real. Could it?

Then the rest of them began jerking, convulsing; their limbs were flying in all directions. Their bodies contorted in ways I could hardly fathom—the fleshy masks stayed firmly attached, but some of them lost legs, arms. Some were nothing but glistening torsos, swelling, and distorting in the unnatural light of the train. I looked on in terror at the grizzly sight in front of me when they all suddenly began moving towards me.

In my utter panic, I turned around and ran. I looked behind me for just a moment and I saw that the mannequins were running too. They were so incredibly *fast.* It was unnatural. I didn't see the door. I hit it head on and stumbled backwards, and then I fell. A sharp, sickening pain travelled through my body—my head felt groggy, full of cotton wool, and my vision blurred.

Before my world turned black, I saw her. I saw Michelle.

She looked skeletal, emaciated and her skin glistened in the bright light. It *sweltered*—just like the others. But she was still human. Her face was still her own. She looked at me and she was crying; her tears shimmered and stained her pastel skin. Her body was bare; naked, but she had something hanging around her neck. It was a sign. My heart sank.

NAME—*Michelle Garcia*

REASON—*Wished for her own brother's death. Resented her own flesh and blood. Unfounded. Discouraging.*

DURATION—*3 years and counting.*

Then everything went dark.

***

When I woke up, I was back on Old Street platform. I looked around and realised that I was on the floor. Curious, worried faces gathered around me as I attempted to assemble my thoughts. Memories of the previous night swirled in my brain like cigarette smoke and seeing Michelle there pained my already fractured heart. I glanced at my watch—it was 8.35am and I had no idea how I got off the train and back to that platform. The reality of seeing real, human faces alleviated the fear and pain that I was feeling somewhat, but I struggled to comprehend the events that took place the previous night.

I've tried to make sense of it ever since it happened—what I saw and what I experienced, but can you ever truly understand something like that? I know I couldn't. I quit drinking after that night—I know that may be difficult to believe, but I did. The encounter gave me purpose, which is something I've never had before and needed desperately—it gave me *hope*. Hope that I will see my sister again.

You see, nothing else matters anymore—only finding Michelle. I will never make the same mistakes again. I don't know who the mannequins were and who put them there, but I vow to find out.

It's 11.44pm and I am at Old Street station, as sober as a dog. It's Wednesday night. Michelle, I'm coming for you and this time, I promise I'll save you.

THE LAST OF HIS KIND

For days, I've followed the dying man through the desert; watching him grow weaker and weaker, unable to help. He must have gotten lost. He's been wandering the desolate land, his life force slowly fading and withering. Much like everything else around here. Including myself.

You see, if I don't eat something soon, I will die. There isn't much to find around here that offers sustenance, and I need to eat. Just like everybody. The body can only go so long without nourishment, and I have already ravaged all the small animals I could find. I have tried so hard not to think about it, but the hunger in my stomach has been gnawing at me, stabbing at me like a jagged edged knife. I don't think I'll be able to hold off for much longer. The man will drop dead soon. I give it a day at the most. He's been dragging himself now, half blind and uttering nonsense under his breath. Not everyone can endure such climates.

I don't normally like to eat human flesh—I am different to my kin. I find the meat too chewy; like eating an uncooked rubbery chicken. It has just never been to my taste, but ever since the disaster—human flesh is all we've had to eat. Me and my kin are the last species to grace this once thriving planet—there are few of us left and pretty soon the food will run out and we too will succumb.

The main reason I've been trying to hold off is because this man, he is the last of his kind. Once he is dead, humanity will be nothing but a memory; a memory that will only remain in the depths of my stomach. When I eat him, that is.

***

The man. He is dead. Death has finally conquered him; he's been laying in the dirt and the waste for a while now. Took longer than I thought, but his suffering is finally over. He lays face down; his body adorned with deep wounds and lacerations. His mouth hangs open; lopsided, and I watch as mucus trickles out onto the grey sand. I moisten my mouth with my serrated tongue; the hunger has remained unrelenting.

I land next to him and sink my clawed feet deep into his stomach. As I take off, something happens that I don't expect. The man, he is still alive. He grips my outstretched wing and pulls; ripping it clean off. We crash headfirst onto the flaked sand.

As I lay, dying. I see a group of humans gathering, their eyes ravenous. I see them holding the heads of what was left of my kin. We underestimated them; they are much stronger than we were; they have endured, and that will has altered them beyond what they once were.

They have replaced us and have now become the Vultures.

THE LITTLE GIRL MADE OF GLASS

Kids can be incredibly cruel, incredibly callous. I guess, as children, we don't always consider the consequences of our actions. Just not something you think about when you're 12 or 13 years old. As a child, you always want to fit in with your peers; no one ever wants to be the odd one out, do they? I certainly didn't. Which is why things happened the way they did.

Glass girl came into our lives during a particularly problematic period. A collective depression is the best way I could describe it. We were all perpetually wounded and generally unhappy with our own existence. Poor Glass girl got the brunt of it.

You see, she was made entirely out of glass. Her skin would sparkle in the bright morning sun, she was blinding to look at sometimes. We'd all have to wear sunglasses in the summer days. As she'd walk, her feet would clatter against the concrete floor; you'd always know when Glass girl was around. She was so fragile, so completely dependent on those around her, but we didn't understand her. She represented our own vulnerability, and we didn't like that.

So, we decided that there was only one thing we could do. We lured her out with promises of kindness and candy; it was a bitter-sweet moment. Her jagged face was a perfect picture of betrayal when she realised what was about to happen to her. She tried to run, but how far can a body made of glass get? Not very.

As we swung the baseball bats across her delicate arms, legs and torso; she cried lead tears. We were destroying her innocence as well as ours. I didn't expect the blood, though; the wine-red fluid poured out of every hole and crevice that we created. For a moment, I was worried that her pain and her gore would stain the carpet, but the stains she left on our hearts were so much more eternal; they were evergreen.

When we were finished, we swept the bloodied fragments, and we discarded them in the nearest bin. We felt elated, like a laden weight had been lifted off our burdening shoulders, because we no longer had to really *feel* anything. We took everything out on Glass girl, and we didn't look back.

***

Jonas was found first, then Maria and then Kate. Small shards of glass were found piercing their coronary arteries. Their hearts broken, splintered. Authorities were baffled, everyone was baffled, but I knew—I *knew* who it was. It's been years, but I never forgot her.

That's why I know that I'm next. I know she'll be coming for me. Ready to pierce and shatter my heart just as I had done hers.

THE CALL

Operator: Nine-one-one operator. What is your emergency?

Caller: I think there is someone outside my house.

Operator: Okay, ma'am. What's your name?

Caller: Cindy.

Operator: Okay, Cindy. Can you tell me what's happening?

Caller: I woke up to this scraping noise, like someone was dragging long fingernails on glass. Then these bright flashing lights started appearing in all my windows simultaneously. Can you please send someone?

Operator: Cindy, what's your location?

Caller: It's 411 Malt Avenue. It's a bright red house, you can't miss it.

Operator: Okay, Cindy. Help is on the way. Do you know if you're alone in the house?

Caller: I-I don't know. I think they're all outside. I can see darkened figures moving out there. All the windows are steamed up. *Oh my god.*

Operator: Cindy, what's happening?

Caller: *(Inaudible.)*

Operator: Cindy? What's going on?

Caller: All this writing just appeared on my windows. Oh my god, please send someone. I'm so scared.

Operator: Cindy, help is not far away. Can you tell me what's written on the windows?

Caller: It says, 'Let us in'.

Operator: Does it say anything else, Cindy?

Caller: No *(Inaudible)*. Oh my god, there is this awful knocking, it's so slow and deliberate. I'm in my room with the door locked and I can still hear it. What the fuck is going on? Where is the police?

Operator: They are coming, Cindy.

Caller: Someone is laughing.

Operator: Cindy, let us in.

Caller: What? What did you say?

A loud crashing sound is heard in the background, followed by a shrill, piercing scream. The line goes dead.

***

A few days later, the flayed body of Cindy Powell was found in the basement of her home; blood decorated the walls. Investigators say Cindy Powell was skinned alive; crude nail marks were found on her mouth, face and eyelids. Her skin was not found at the scene and has not yet been located by investigators. Police are baffled, and the community shaken.

POKÉMON GO

I've been obsessed with playing Pokémon Go ever since its release in 2016. I've loved Pokémon since I was a kid, though—playing the original games and watching the cartoons. It was just something that I loved doing along with my boyfriend—Daniel. He and I would spend all our free time walking in parks around our local area. It might seem sad and pathetic to some of you, and I guess it is, but it was our thing; something we bonded over and something that brought us closer together. If I knew what would happen years down the line, I'd have deleted the app long ago, but I didn't. You only live to regret shit after it has already happened. Life's a bastard like that sometimes.

After a while, the game slowly lost its allure, and I stopped playing for a while; both of us did. I think life just got in the way you know—new jobs, new responsibilities. All that boring jazz. We didn't pick the game back up until quite recently, a few months ago now. Although, it seems like everything happened only yesterday. It all seems so very raw still, like a wound that hasn't quite healed and has become infected; necrotic. It's been slowly eating away at me. But the gangrenous wound is on the inside and not something that I can just chuck a plaster on; it's etched so deep into my soul that I don't know that I'll ever truly get over it. Maybe talking about it will help.

Daniel and I were in bed one day, so long ago now, watching some nondescript TV show that I can't even remember the name of. Both of us were just unwinding on our phones, as most couples do in the 21st century, I guess. I was swiping through my apps when I saw that I had a notification on the Pokémon Go app. Absentmindedly, I clicked it; realising how long it's been since I played. When it eventually loaded, I was greeted by the familiar bright colours of the game itself. My character stood amongst the cartoon streets, surrounded by poke stops and gyms. We always got lucky with our location, as it was a hot spot for Pokémon. I had not been logged in for more than 5 minutes before a wild Charmander appeared. I clicked on him, feeling that same familiar excitement that I used to get when playing the game.

When he loaded, I noticed something. There was something different about this Charmander. Usually, he was bright red and vibrant, a normal cartoon animal really. If you can call them animals? Anyway, this one looked... off. He still had the same vibrant colours, but they seemed darker somewhat; more sinister. The orange was mixed with a deep red that appeared almost bloodstained and he was completely adorned in stitches, as if someone carved him open and then stitched him back up crudely with a blunt needle. Instead of the usual ocean blue, his eyes were as black as the night. It kind of creeped me out, so I showed it to Daniel.

"Must be a new update," he said, not even glancing at my phone.

"It doesn't look right though, kinda creepy." I said.

Daniel didn't say anything in response. I sighed, still looking at the Pokémon.

I closed the app, but before I did, I could have sworn that the Charmander smiled at me.

***

A few inconsequential days passed, and I had almost forgotten my encounter with the bizarre Charmander. But one night a few days later, everything in my life changed. I was lying in bed when I suddenly got an overwhelming desire to open the app; I can't explain why, I just really wanted to play the game. Something inside me was willing me to play the game; I don't know what it was. Maybe it was the longing for that old life; the life where Daniel and I didn't have any cares or worries.

I loaded it up and waited patiently for any kind of Pokémon to appear. There was nothing. I waited and waited—minutes turned into an hour and that hour turned into two. Eventually, something spawned—a Cubone. The lonely Pokémon stared at me, holding his signature fragment of cartilage. Nothing seemed untoward or different about him at first glance but upon closer inspection, I noticed that the bone in his hand was stained with blood. I frowned, but before I could do anything, a notification appeared at the top of the page.

Try this with AR! A never-before-seen experience!

I clicked on it, and it immediately showed me my own bedroom. Cubone stood on the floor between my TV and my bed, but he seemed closer this time, like he'd moved a few inches toward me. I decided to play along and catch him. Maybe this was just some new, creepy as fuck update that they were trying out. I clicked into my inventory and noticed that all the Poke balls looked different too; they were different shapes than the usual oval. They were square with jagged edges.

Weird.

I picked one and, with a somewhat shaky finger, I spun the ball and threw it at the Cubone. The ball quivered and shook, but the Cubone stayed in. Afterwards, I stared at the screen—the augmented reality was still active, but there were no Pokémon to catch. However, I thought I could see something in the open doorway of my room. I thought I saw something that was in the shape of a face. Long, dark and scraggly hair obscured the features, but I could see two pairs of glowing eyes; they burned bright like the morning sun. What the fuck was this?

I was certain this wasn't part of the experience, and it freaked me out. I tried to zoom in on the face, but I couldn't. Looking at it filled me with such dread. I wanted to show it to Daniel, though, so I took a screenshot. I turned to face him, but he was already asleep. With a disquieted sigh, I quit the app and tried to go to sleep.

I should have left it well enough alone.

***

The next morning, I tried to explain what I saw to Daniel—who, as per his usual, reacted with indifference. It annoyed me, so I tried to show him the screenshot but when I opened my photo album, there was nothing there.

"You probably dreamt it," he said, not taking his eyes off his phone to even look at me.

"Fuck you, Daniel. I know what I saw." I said and stormed out of the room.

I was incredibly shaken. Was it possible that I could have dreamt it? I couldn't get that haunting face out of my mind, though; those eyes burned deep into my soul. It was real. I went back to our bedroom, and I launched the app once more. I was greeted with the familiar loading screen and when the game appeared, instead of the cartoon world, I saw my own bedroom again. I tried to quit the augmented reality, but I couldn't. They say curiosity kills the cat and now I believe in that phrase more than anything.

I looked around the room—everything looked normal and un-changed, on the surface at least. I continued looking around the room, hoping to see something—I don't know why I wanted to see something, I just did. Then suddenly everything... changed. My room was still my room, but it looked different—everything was so dark, like the sun had been swallowed. The floor was stained, a mixture of blood and dirt. Everything looked *old*, so old. My heart leaped into my mouth when I saw two figures standing in the doorway. They were clad in ripped, threadbare rags and covered in blood. It dripped from every orifice onto the floor. *I knew who they were.*

It was Daniel and me.

I whimpered, utterly frozen by fear. I tried to call out Daniel's name, but all I could muster was a small, faint wail. That was when they both turned to look at me. I lowered the phone and when I did, I saw that everything looked normal; I could see Daniel's silhou-ette on the laminated flooring. I glanced back at my phone. The two figures were now facing me, and our eyes met. Their faces were bloated and bulbous. Neither of them had a mouth; only two bright, glowing eyes.

I heard someone calling my name—I knew that it was coming from my phone, but the faint, robotic sound echoed around my room and in my head. The voice sounded scratchy, guttural; like someone had been scraping razor blades on their vocal cords. Hesitantly, I picked up the phone, and I saw her face; the face that was supposed to be mine. The blank space where her mouth was supposed to be suddenly ripped open. Blood, teeth and viscera splattered across the screen. The now gaping hole oozed crimson; like a sudden dam had broken inside. She was moving her mouth as if she wanted to say something, but the blood just wouldn't relent; it kept flowing. I dropped my phone when I saw my own hands—they were covered in fresh, glistening blood.

I finally managed to scream. I screamed for Daniel, but he didn't come. I rushed out to the kitchen and what I saw then, I will never forget. I saw Daniel's phone on the floor with his body halfway submerged inside the screen. I couldn't make myself move. I tried so hard, I screamed at my muscles to move, but they wouldn't. I stood helplessly as that thing that was meant to be Daniel pulled *my* Daniel inside that blood filled, sunless world. By the time I was able to move, the deed had been done. Daniel was gone. I ran to his phone, but it was blank; broken.

I turned to face my own room, and I looked at the phone that lay on my bed. Before I went back in, I retrieved the sharpest knife that I could find in my kitchen. I stabbed the phone incessantly until the screen was nothing but shattered glass.

***

I never saw Daniel again. He was declared missing; I was a suspect for a while, naturally, but eventually I was cleared due to lack of evidence. I moved away, and I tried to never look back, tried so hard, but it has proven to be difficult. I dream about the day Daniel was sucked into that awful, horrendous world and I dream about that other *me.* The one with the never-ending bleeding mouth and glowing eyes.

I haven't played Pokémon Go since; the phone I have now doesn't support the app and I am thankful for that because some days, I yearn to see what I saw as much as it terrified me. I desperately wanted to find Daniel, though—I wanted to save him.

I haven't been the same since and I know that I can't be saved, but please, I beg you, don't play Pokémon Go. You don't know what you'll find.

THEY'RE IN THE BLOOD

Have you ever felt your blood move? I don't just mean flowing through your veins like a crimson river, transporting life to your vital organs. No, that's not what I mean. I guess you can't really feel that, anyway. No, what I'm trying to convey here, it's something different. Something downright fucking unnatural.

I have been seeing my veins *move* and warp in ways they shouldn't. I'd lay in bed for hours, just watching them distort, thinking myself deformed. I'd see bulbous little shapes form underneath my skin, *human* shapes. I know how that sounds, believe me, I do, but it's true. It almost seemed like something was crawling through my blood vessels, sending a fiery pain through my body. My nerve endings felt like they were being torn out and shredded. Have you ever accidentally put your hand in a blender? That's what it felt like.

I didn't want to go to the doctor or anything, though. I mean, what would I even say? *"Hey Doc, I think I've got people living in my blood. Fancy helping me out?"* It sounds ridiculous, right? It's fucking stupid. No, I didn't go, and I guess maybe I should have, because things only got worse.

One morning, I woke up covered in blood. My right arm was completely submerged; wet and glossy. Underneath, my flesh was in pieces; torn up like bits of old tissue. But that wasn't what sent a dagger through my heart, no. Leading away into my crimson-coloured sheets were tiny, bloody footsteps. My other arm quivered. I hesitated before uncovering the sheet, wondering what the fuck I'd find under it.

I discarded the sheet—ripped off the band aid, as they say. Underneath, my bed was saturated. I wondered how much blood

I'd lost. My mind felt foggy, as if stuffed with cotton wool. Scattered amidst the bloody sheets were miniature pitchforks, knives, and an axe. Shit that I couldn't explain. The thing that turned my blood turned to ice though, was the message.

"Do you feel us?"

And I *could* feel them.

My body hummed with pain and my skin bubbled, melting away like candle wax. It leaked onto my already blood-soaked sheets, conjuring up some abhorrent fleshy cocktail. Then I felt my stomach split open, as seamlessly as buttons on a shirt. I peeked inside the meaty crevice, the blood gushing like a fountain. Inside, I saw thousands of them. *The little people that lived in my blood.*

I could feel myself fading, but before my world went black, one of them approached me. It was smiling, a detestable smile that spread from ear to ear. Its blood-soaked skin glistened as it climbed onto my torn chin, discarding bits of my sinewy tissue that hung limply to its face.

"Your baby's flesh will accommodate us for years to come." It said, its teeth were sharp, like daggers.

I didn't even know that I was pregnant.

MY DAUGHTER

I don't know when the disappearances began. Perhaps it was 2 months into the summer holidays, perhaps it was a few weeks. I really couldn't say. The time frames really have no bearing anymore. It didn't appear to be anything too concerning at first, but when more and more kids started vanishing, our small-knit community was shaken. Police, parents and a handful of volunteers started organising searches. Their despair was painfully apparent, and the futility of the situation was… harsh, to say the least. I was fearful for my daughter, Norma. It didn't affect her in the slightest, though.

I remember being so busy preparing for Norma's birthday—it was the big 12. Norma said, *"it was her most important day"* She was obsessed that summer. All she would talk about for months was how spectacular this birthday was going to be. How it was going to be one to remember. I had no idea how right she would be. It felt wrong somehow though—to be celebrating when all these horrific things were happening all around us. Norma didn't care though, if anything, she was happier than she'd ever been. It was quite spine-chilling, to tell you the truth.

She became more and more… manic. With each passing day, I would wake up to my wide-eyed daughter babbling on about how this was going to be the best birthday that anyone could ever dream of. I sort of laughed it off at first, you know. I mean, I wasn't planning anything extravagant. After all, she was only 12.

Her birthday was about a month away when the smell hit. I couldn't figure out what it was—it was sweet and sickly, like meat that had been left out in the sun for too long. It overwhelmed the house. Every crevice and every bit of lone furniture devoured the smell. No matter how much I cleaned, I could still smell it. Hiding underneath the scent of the lemony bleach. It lingered in the air like a soft summer cloud. I could never work out the source of the smell, as it seemed to seep out from every corner in every room. It was both strong and weak. It was always more pungent in Norma's room, though.

Besides the smell, other things started happening. Strange, unidentifiable noises would plague our house in the night. Footsteps that sounded like they were coming from *inside* the walls. Slow, barely audible scratches that emanated from each room. I had shrugged it off at first, maybe thinking we had a rat infestation, but when I started finding stray bits of hair—that was when the fear really started to seep in. I would find strands of all colours, just casually strewn around the house; nothing that would be alarming to a normal person, but Norma and I had brown hair. Why was I finding blonde and black hairs? Every day, I would find new hairs tucked away in the little nooks and crannies of my house.

I couldn't figure out where they were coming from.

I stopped sleeping eventually. My mind was in perpetual disarray. Desperately trying to figure out *who* was leaving these hairs, what this smell was, and generally yearning to discover what was happening in my house.

Norma seemed to notice none of it. Still just too preoccupied with her upcoming birthday. *"You'll see, Daddy"*, she'd say.

I thought I was going mad.

Norma's birthday was fast approaching, and things only proved to intensify, worsen. By now, half of Norma's class had disappeared, and everyone was at a complete loss. Norma was spending more and more time locked up in her bedroom—I'd hear her whispering at night. Her low, hushed voice echoed in the silence of our house. Sometimes I could have sworn I heard someone else in there with her—a man, but when I'd burst in, Norma would be completely alone. Sitting in the darkness with her eyes wide, glistening like two little pale moons.

On the day of Norma's birthday, I was still wholly distracted by the smell and the sounds that seemed to be taking over my house, my life. I couldn't find Norma and I couldn't find any of the balloons, cake or presents that I had prepared the night before. Confused, I made my way to her bedroom. When I entered, she wasn't there, but her wardrobe door was the first thing that I noticed. It was ajar. The smell was stronger than ever. As I got closer, I saw that the back of the wardrobe inside was hollow, revealing a secret passage.

I was terrified by this point. My mind was overwrought with thoughts. Since when did we have a trap door? Since when did my house have a secret fucking room in the walls? I had to find Norma, though, so I made my way inside. Fuck me, the smell. It was Herculean back here. I could hear a faint, low voice, guttural in sound. A man was singing Happy Birthday inside my walls.

I entered the small room. I recoiled at the sight that beseeched all my senses. Around a small circular table were all the missing kids. Party hats of all colours adorned their rotting, balding scalps. Their throats were split open. Their intestines lay strewn on the table, their insides replaced with rainbow cake. Some of them were fresher than others.

"My god, Norma. What have you done?" I stammered.

A wide, crimson smile spread across her deranged face. "Daddy, I told you. Don't you see? This birthday is going to last forever. *He* said so."

***

I lost my daughter that day, she just vanished. *Into thin air.* That's the best way I can describe it. All I was left with was a party hat and a whole bunch of dead kids. Did the police suspect me? Of course, they did, but I wasn't the one that was missing. My daughter was, and they sought her out more than they did me. The families of those children got closure, which I guess was cathartic for me in some way—despite my own predicaments.

I have dedicated my life to trying to find my daughter, but I never did find out who *he* was.

PICTURE PERFECT

I've always believed my family was picture perfect, doesn't everyone? I guess it's a cliche, but it's the truth in my case. My wife and child are my world, always have been. Recently though, my family hasn't been acting quite like themselves. Or at least not how I remember them.

My whole *world* hasn't been acting quite like it should, or at least not how I remember it. I've been experiencing these flashbacks—memories that I don't think are mine. They can't be. I keep seeing myself driving a car with my wife and daughter beside me, laughing idly.

I've never driven a car before.

Then it's followed by conversations with people I don't know, people I had never seen before—men in white coats and perfectly ironed cheap suits. I don't know what they're saying, but they surround me, pity in their eyes. Their words are always just out of my reach, always too incoherent for me to grasp—like voices underwater.

My wife and daughter have been watching me when I sleep lately. It wakes me up—that feeling of having eyes burning into the back of your skull. They both stand there, their eyes devoid of any emotion; hollow. Their faces are expressionless—not a touch of humanity graces their blank features.

It was unsettling.

The memories have been getting more and more intense lately. I see the same thing almost daily. The car, the doctors, the men in suits. I can't shake the feeling that these memories are somehow *mine* and that I have lived them before, but how could this be? How would I have forgotten such events?

I have been overcome by this bottomless, awful feeling of un-imaginable grief—like I'd experienced something traumatic. What, I didn't know.

My wife and daughter have been acting stranger and stranger too. I've noticed how *unnatural* their movements are. Mechanical and jerky. They seemed almost *robotic*. Their skin glistened abnormally, looked artificial almost.

The memories flooded my brain as if on a loop. I had begun hearing fragmented voices when they replayed in my head.

"We're so sorry for your loss Mr Blanch."

Sorry for my loss? What had I lost?

Then one night, it hit me. *That night.* Monica, Lucy and I were in a car and I was driving. I looked away for a split second, *just a second.* That's all it took for the other car to hit us. I remember watching as Monica's neck snapped like a twig in the seat beside me. Lucy's fragile, little body snapped in half as the force of the impact became apparent.

"They died instantly." They told me.

"It was painless." They said.

Can death ever be painless?

"We can help you, Mr Blanch."

"We can give you your family back and take your pain away. Take your memories away."

They didn't give me back what I lost. They gave me an *artificial* picture-perfect family instead.

THE TEST SUBJECT IN ROOM 25

I was awoken by a meek squeaking sound. When I opened my eyes, I saw that I was surrounded by cages—each one occupied by these hairy, repugnant beasts. Rats. They were all staring at me, hunger plaguing their eyes. Any movement I made was met with a hiss, the buzz of starvation.

I didn't know where I was. Last thing I remember was watching TV in my front room, then seeing this blinding white light and then… nothing. Until I woke up here.

"Commencing Test."

I looked around, trying to seek out the source of the voice. It sounded like it was coming from everywhere, all at once. My mind raced, I couldn't figure out what was going on. I felt groggy and not myself. Panic threatened to engulf me like waves of a stormy ocean.

"Let me go, please." That was all I could muster.

"Release specimen one."

As soon as the phantom voice uttered those words, a latch was released on one of the cages. It was the biggest rat I had ever seen; its eyes a deep crimson. Its mouth was agape and from within it emerged a saturated, serrated tongue. Its teeth were as sharp as nails, covered in some sort of brown substance that glistened in the dim light.

Before I could do anything, it launched itself at me. Tearing at the exposed skin of my leg. It chewed and crunched the muscle, the sinewy tissue—it looked like plasticine inside the creature's mouth.

"Release all specimens." Uttered the voice.

At that moment, I heard all the catches release at once; it was almost musical. The rats surrounded me, snarling. The scent of my blood lingered in the air. The rats moved closer and closer to my face. I stiffened, not knowing what to do, and before I could move, they all threw themselves at my fear-stricken face.

I felt my skin loosen as they tore into it—it came apart as easily as ripe, cooked meat. The pain was unimaginable, searing. It was as if all my nerve endings were set ablaze. I writhed in agony as they ripped me apart at the seams, sunk their teeth into my exposed muscle. The blood poured out of me like molten lava, covering me head to toe.

"Test Terminated"

That was the last thing I heard before the world turned black.

***

EXPERIMENT NOTES

When we landed on this planet, we wanted to find out what made humans tick. We yearned to learn about what made them *feel* and we wanted to know if this fervour burned within their souls. We have yet to discover more beyond the flesh. The next test subject in room 30 is submerged in water. We want to see how long it takes for a human to drown. Findings to follow…

MISSING FINGERS

I think it was a Wednesday when I first noticed that the third finger on my right hand was missing. There was no wound, no blood, no scarring. It was just gone, disappeared. Poof! Into thin air my finger went. I could still *feel* its presence though. When I'd look at my delicately manicured fingers, I wouldn't see it, but I'd feel it. Phantom limb syndrome, they call it right?

I went out of my mind with fright. How was this possible? How could my finger just disappear? This wasn't right. Where was all the blood? It looked as if I had never had a finger there in the first place. I had no idea where it went. I tried looking for it too, in the most obvious places. Had I accidentally lost it in my sofa? Like when you lose a few coins and somehow, they always end up in the deep recesses of your couch. It's a whole different universe that just swallows your shit without your knowledge. My finger wasn't in the sofa though. It wasn't in my freezer, either. It just felt so innocuous; it's positively the stupidest fucking thing that could have happened to me, to anyone.

I went to the emergency room, convinced that I'd possibly lost my fucking mind, but when I got there, they told me that the third finger on my right hand was perfectly fine, intact, in fact. Was I going through some sudden episode of psychosis? They thought it was some sort of joke, that I was taking the piss and threatened to call the police if I didn't leave—telling me I should go see a psychiatrist. I left, fingerless and alone, going out of my mind. When did this happen? When did I suddenly lose grip on reality? I knew I hadn't lost my marbles; I knew that they were still rolling around in my head, undamaged, alert and definitely fucking solid.

But *something* was happening to me. Fingers don't just disappear for no reason.

I tried to make peace with the loss of my finger, though; *just forget about it*, I'd think to myself.

For a while, I did. It sort of worked. I went to see a psychiatrist, who also told me that the third finger on my right hand was indeed still attached." *If it was still attached, then why the fuck can't I see it?"* I'd demand. I'd scream and shout. I was getting nowhere. No one was helping me. If anything, I felt even more insane and even more frightened. Even my family wouldn't believe me.

Other bizarre things started happening in my apartment. I started hearing peculiar and just completely unfuckingexplainable noises all hours of the day. They all seemed to emanate from *inside* my sofa. From inside my walls, too. I'd hear scratching noises, like someone was scraping long, hard fingernails on glass. It was constant, piercing, and it felt like my eardrums were being obliterated by a cheese grater.

A manic buzzing sound resonated from my sofa, as if a fly was stuck underneath a blanket, but when I'd search it, there would be nothing there, no fly. Nothing. Most disturbingly of all, I'd hear the cries of a baby. The cries would increase in volume, becoming horribly unbearable and when they were on the verge of reducing me to a blubbering mess; they would cease as quickly as they started.

Little did I know that things would only get worse, only intensify, and I felt utterly helpless. I had no one to talk to, had no one there to help me.

It all threatened to engulf me fully when I woke up a few days later to find that three more fingers on my right hand were gone. I mean, this was getting fucking ridiculous. I pulled my apartment apart to the very core, and I searched the interior. I knew that *something* was doing this to me. There were so many random holes that lead to butt fuck nowhere and no, I still couldn't find my fingers.

I rummaged in my sofa one more time. It is a place that will consume everything you give it, so I figured maybe if I looked properly, I'd find them. I knew there was something seriously fucking wrong with this sofa. I discarded the throw, the pillows and put my hand in that bottomless pit. It went as far as my shoulder, but I couldn't feel anything finger shaped inside. I scoured the black hole until I felt something soft, a blanket. I pulled it out, and I felt a pang in my chest, a lump in my throat. It smelled like baby powder and something inside me told me that I recognised it, that I knew it, but my brain synapses just wouldn't click together. I contemplated climbing inside, but I was scared I would never come back out again.

Every day for a week, the rest of my fingers would get just that little bit smaller, shrinking in size. Until they would completely disappear. By the end of that week, I had just five and a half fingers left out of ten. When I noticed that it started affecting my toes, I knew that I didn't have long left. Whatever it was, it was consuming me whole and soon I would cease to exist.

A few nights later, I woke up to an overwhelming feeling of being pulled. A squelching noise reached my ears as I opened my eyes. I saw my right hand, its remaining fingers inside the mouth of what looked like a baby. Those brain synapses finally snapped together like the mouth of a snapping turtle. *This is my baby, the one I put in the sofa.* He had the body of a man but the head of a new-born baby. The umbilical cord was tied around his neck, giving him a plum, deathly hue. His hands were small and pudgy, and they gripped my thumb, *chewing and sucking.* I think I remember just screaming my lungs out. I tried to tear myself away from him, from *it,* but his grip was so strong, so incredibly powerful. His grotesque and mutilated body writhed and squirmed on the bed next to me.

He looked up and a raspy, gravelly voice escaped his wet lips.

"Now it's your turn to be inside me, Mamma."

SHIPWRECKED

Day 2. 10.30am.

We have just finished going through the resources in the small boat that we escaped on. There are four of us, Phil, a quiet, balding and perturbed retired professor. Sandra, a jittery, tearful blonde, apparently a schoolteacher pre-disaster. Polly, an OCD freak, secretary at a law firm. She's been perched on a log ever since we got here, unmoving.

Then, there is me. I work as a janitor in a hospital and lead a thrill-free, tedious life. I'm in no rush to escape, not yet anyway.

Day 3. 9.30am.

The morning on an uninhabited island is certainly beautiful. Everything is untouched and unsoiled by an intentionally damaging human hand. Of course, now that we are here, everything is different, the island is somehow different. It is no longer pure and no longer untamed. I think I'm the only one awake now. I picked the most detached spot. The palm trees stand still in the absence of wind being scorched by the hot sun, the huge rocks and derelict logs stand along the sandy beach with a few of the survivors scattered, looking misplaced.

Soon the others begin to stir.

9.55pm.

Smoke! There is smoke coming from the woods! Sandra yelped about half an hour ago about some sort of black fog coming out of the woods. We were all in the process of dozing off for the night when the most ear-splitting squeal escaped her stupid, self-centred mouth.

Once she calmed down, I suggested that we all split up and investigate.

Day 3. 11.30pm.

I was the first to get back, grasping my dimming flashlight tightly in my quivering hand, my body and mind overwhelmed with fear and confusion. How could it be? How could it be possible that all four of us perceived the same image in the desolate woods? My hand is trembling violently now. I grip the pencil firmly in my sweating palm, struggling to keep it steady on the page. The woods are empty and hollow. No signs of a fire were apparent when I discovered the place the smoke derived from.

Are we all finally going insane? Images of blood, flesh and carnage flash in my mind as my breathing fastens—I see Polly, her eye gouged out, tongue protruding out of her pain-stricken mouth. I see my face, a manic smile embracing my blood-splattered face. My tubby hand clasps a butcher's knife, stained with old and new blood—it drips onto the sandy floor, clotting the yellowness as it absorbs the thick liquid.

I look around me. Three bodies lay slain on the beach, eviscerated, cut up and executed—by me. I close my eyes. I hear voices in the distance. I feel the icy steel cooling my sweat covered palm. The bitter feel of the blade startles me, and I open my eyes. A knife. I know what I must do now.

I FUCKING HATE MUSHROOMS

Can I just start this off by saying that I fucking hate mushrooms, always have. It's just something about their rubbery texture that always puts me off; it's like chewing boot leather. Don't even get me started on the taste—like eating raw earth. I can't stomach it.

My brother hasn't been answering my calls recently. I never had a great relationship with him to begin with, but still, he was my brother, and I was worried. I decided to go by his house, see what I could find. When I got there, I found the most bizarre thing on his dining room table—a mushroom. It was so perfectly placed, like a present. My brother wasn't there.

I approached it tentatively, wary of its obtrusive presence. Like a bomb that was about to explode. As I neared, I noticed how grotesque it was. These bulbous lumps protruded, resembling infected tumours. It was covered in blocked pores—these gnarled little holes that oozed something unidentifiable. I had never seen a mushroom like that. As I stood before it, this strange scent travelled up my nostrils; it was sweet, yet earthy. It smelled *good*. I was suddenly famished. That feeling you get when you haven't eaten in days. Something inside me *needed* to eat this mushroom. I couldn't explain it.

My hand reached out and touched the exterior—it felt rough, jagged and sharp. Before I could stop myself, I snatched the thing in my hands and shoved it hungrily into my mouth. It tasted *wonderful*, like eating all your favourite things at once. My taste buds exploded. It was glorious.

A few days passed, the sublime taste of that mushroom still lingered and endured—it was all I could think about. The worries for my missing brother had all but vanished. Then I noticed that my arms were adorned in holes of various sizes—some were big, some small. All were oozing pus and blood—thick and slimy. I stared at them, horrified.

Then I started growing stems; my fingernails, my toenails—everything was replaced by a mushroom head. From within my crimson-coloured holes sprouted spores, out of which *thousands* of other little mushrooms emerged, my blood had turned to soil. Pretty soon, I was covered from head to toe by these grotesque things.

I think I know what happened to my brother.

***

I've laid here for days now, willing myself to die, but somehow, I was still here, and I was a mushroom. I hear footsteps and the sounds of a key turning. Somehow, I can still see.

It's my mother. She visits on Tuesdays. I watch as she edges closer toward me, confused by the sight of me.

"What's this? A mushroom?" I hear her say.

"Oh, I love mushrooms!" Her hands reach out, she grasps me in her sweaty palms and lifts me into her gaping mouth.

GUILT IS TANGIBLE

"Shh, Mr Caprish, it's ok. I'm right here." I whispered to him as he lay on his bed, gripping my hand weakly.

"Not long now. The pain will be gone soon." I had hoped that my voice soothed him, that it provided some sort of reprieve from the pain I knew he was feeling. It probably didn't, but hope was the only thing that kept me going in this job.

There wasn't anything I could do for him. There wasn't anything I could do for *any* of them. I was there to provide emotional support to those knocking on death's door. To those that were long past any medical intervention—to those for whom death was the only possible answer, the only solution.

"Is Babs here?" He whispered to me, his voice meek and silent. The cancer had completely savaged his eyesight, as well as his memory. He had forgotten that his wife was long gone, buried deep in the earth. My heart broke for him. I did what most people would do in my position—I lied.

"Yes, Mr Caprish. Babs is here. She's right by your side." I caressed his frail hand. The skin felt crumpled and dry like paper. I looked down and examined our hands as they lay on his bed, intertwined. Mine were smooth yet worn and his were rough, ravaged by age; adorned in liver spots.

Pretty soon, the inevitable happened. He closed his eyes, mouth agape; teeth all but yellowed and crumbled. I watched as his chest rose up and down, completely in sync; slow but steady, and then it stopped. Just like that, Mr Caprish was dead. There was no one left to cry but me—he didn't have any children and all his other family was dead. There was no one left to grieve, and I *did* grieve. The sorrow doesn't deplete with time, if anything, it elevates—gets stronger and more intense. Can you imagine what it's like to die completely alone? No, I bet you can't. This is why I exist.

I might as well get this bit out of the way. I'm a death mid-wife—another more common term for it is a death doula. It's not the sort of job I imagined myself to be in, but we never do, do we? We never end up doing what we thought we would. Death doulas require little to no medical experience—our whole purpose is to provide spiritual and/or emotional support to those moments from death. Those terminally ill patients that are past hospice care or those that have no families. You'd be surprised how many are affected by the latter.

The job itself was unrelenting—you couldn't hang on to your emotions for too long after you lost a patient because there was no room for pause. Time would lose all its authority. Death didn't wait.

Shortly after the death of Mr Caprish, I was assigned another terminally ill patient. His name was Allen Rose. I didn't know too much about him at the time—aside from his debilitating illness and the fact that he didn't have a family. Apparently, Mr Rose had been given five days to live, and he specifically asked for a death doula to assist him in his passing.

A few days later, I found myself standing outside his house. It was on the outskirts of town. I won't say where because I don't want anyone knowing where I'm from, so I'll keep that bit vague. The house itself was moderately sized, big enough for a family of three. I took a moment to examine it—it looked extremely run down. The maroon brick crumbled and flaked, the windows were covered in filth and the whole house oozed abandonment.

"You must be Miriam." Came the pleasant voice of the visiting nurse.

"Yes. Miriam Plateu." I said, extending my hand.

She shook it, albeit hesitantly and stepped aside.

"I'm Katherine. All yours." She said.

I walked in and was immediately struck by the crisp air; my skin felt like it was being assaulted by small, sharp icicles. The lights were dim, and I found myself squinting to see.

"Yeah, he doesn't like the light. You staying the full five days?" She asked.

"Yes, however long it takes." I replied. Her eyes surveyed me; I could feel the scorn in them. There were some nurses that didn't respect the profession I was in. Especially since I had barely any medical training. To them, I was just a glorified therapist.

"He's refusing all meds now, so I don't need to come back, but if the pain gets too bad, just call me. I don't live far." She said, barely looking at me.

"Here, let me show you through." She said. I could tell she wanted this exchange to be over as quickly as possible and truth be told, so did I.

We walked through the darkened hallway, and I found myself looking around. The house was bigger inside than it looked on the outside; the interior was unkempt, but I could tell it was once very well lived in. As I passed each room, I noticed various items strewn around the floor—a teddy bear, a few items of clothing that I deduced belonged to a woman in her late 30s. Items that you wouldn't expect a man living alone to have. *He must have had a family at some point. What happened to them?* I found myself wondering.

"Mr Rose, Miriam Plateu is here." The voice of the nurse brought me back to reality.

Judging by the utter disarray of the room, I could tell that Allen Rose was confined entirely to his bed. My eyes travelled toward his frail body, and I almost gasped when I saw him. I composed myself, but it was difficult swallowing the man's ghastly frame.

He was extremely emaciated, looking almost skeletal. His head was bereft of hair; it glistened in the dim light. It looked as smooth as the skin of a newborn baby; pristine and without blemishes. The rest of him though... His skin looked loose, like it didn't quite fit him. It almost seemed like he was wearing a fleshy suit. It was the colour of old parchment paper; yellow and tainted.

As I studied Mr Rose, something else caught my eye. Something shone and gleamed under him, surrounding him like a shrine. As I looked closer, I almost recoiled in disgust. It was a black substance that I had never seen before—it was congealed to his sheets, glued to his skin. It looked thick, sticky, and it *glowed*. I looked around at the nurse in a panic, opened my mouth to speak, but then closed it again when I saw that she was looking at Mr Rose like I was, but she wasn't *seeing* what I was. I didn't want to sound unhinged—so I didn't utter a word.

"Is there anything else you need from me?" She asked, looking nonchalant, irritated.

"No, nothing." I murmured and watched as she sauntered out of the room. Not a care in a world.

Once I heard the door slam, my gaze fell back upon Mr Rose and the strange, black goo that surrounded him.

"Hi Mr Rose. I'm Mirriam Plateu and I'm from Restful Retreat. You requested someone from our company to… help you." When I spoke, my voice sounded unnatural. It concerned me further because I wasn't a newb, I've done this hundreds of times. But something about Allen Rose and his situation unnerved me.

He opened his eyes a little and looked at me. His stare was blank, emotionless, *cold.* It sent shivers down my spine. When he finally spoke, his voice sounded rough, like he'd swallowed razor blades.

"So you're the death doula?" He asked.

"Yes, Mr Rose. My name's Miriam. Is there anything you need me to do for you?" I asked.

"All I want you to do is listen to what I have to say. Nothing else." He said. His eyes were closed now. I was surprised by his harsh tone.

"Of course, Mr Rose. That's what I'm here for." I said, walking closer.

"Sit down then. I don't have long left."

I fumbled with my hands, feeling awkward, and took one of the nearby chairs and sat down. I felt like a petulant child, being told off and sent to detention. I sat down and watched him, averting my eyes. He made me nervous.

"I'm listening, Mr Rose." I managed to stammer.

"Do you know that guilt isn't metaphorical? It's a very real, very tangible thing and it can literally *consume* you." He began.

"Sorry, I'm not sure what you mean?" I asked.

"Please let me speak." He said.

I bowed my head, feeling ashamed. What was wrong with me? I knew it wasn't me that was supposed to do the talking. I was there to simply listen and only answer when needed, when prompted.

"I used to have a family. A wife and son that I loved dearly. They meant the world to me; they were my everything." He continued.

"What happened to them?" I asked. I could hear the fear in my voice. I imagined he could, too.

"I'll get to that." He said, lifting his quivering hands to his weather-beaten face.

"It was all my fault…" He trailed off.

"What was your fault, Mr Rose? What happened?" I asked.

He didn't speak for a moment and my eyes travelled back toward the mysterious goo. It seemed to have doubled in size since I first spotted it—almost tripled. As I peered closer, I noticed that it was fused with his skin. I opened my mouth to speak.

"Mr Rose. W-what is…?"

Then I saw it *move*. It began pulsating, throbbing almost, and it emanated this peculiar smell. It stung my nostrils, and I had to cover my nose, albeit discreetly. It was sour, pungent—like expired milk. The aroma hung in the air like death. It was ironic, really. Mr Rose cut the silence with his gruff voice and continued speaking, completely ignoring my question and the puzzled look that enveloped my face.

"The night it happened was just like any other night, you know? It's amazing how many things you take for granted. We had just gotten back from the cinema; I can't even remember the film we went to see. Something Troy liked, probably. Moira was preparing Troy's lunch for the following morning, and I settled in my office for the evening. I worked for a couple of hours and before I knew it, I passed out."

He took a deep breath. I could see that he was struggling—the sweat poured down his face like water from a broken tap.

"Do you need to take a break, Mr Rose? How's your pain?" I interjected.

He ignored my question.

"When I woke up, it was a little after midnight. My eyes were blurry, and my head felt like it was filled with cotton wool. My temples throbbed, and I rubbed them to try and alleviate the discomfort I was suddenly feeling. I looked around and noticed how dark it was. The silence made me nervous. If anything, it was *too* quiet. I remember this anxiety washing over me and I couldn't understand where it came from." His voice began quivering.

"What did you do?" I found myself asking.

"I became worried, so I decided to check on my wife and son. I wanted to make sure they were ok. I know how ridiculous that may sound. Why wouldn't they be ok? But I don't know, I just felt like *something* wasn't quite right. I didn't know what at that moment, though."

"I walked out into the hallway and that was when I heard it...the crying. It was coming from downstairs, so I followed it. I walked carefully, slowly. For some reason, I didn't want to be heard. Something about that small wail terrified me. The house was dark, but the dim lights from downstairs illuminated the way for me. As I neared the bottom, I saw them."

"Who?" I asked.

"*Them.* They stood in a circle, encircling something. I couldn't see what it was at first, but as I got closer, I saw that it was Moira and Troy. They were tied up and gagged. Then I saw something gleam in the faint light and it dawned on me that it was a knife. They were clad all in black. Their long, thick robes touched the floor. They wore masks that covered the entirety of their faces. They were metallic, from what I could see. Not like any masks I'd ever seen. One of them held a knife to my wife's throat and muttered something. I couldn't hear what it was. She began shaking her head violently. Tears streamed down her ruby-red cheeks. Then her eyes darted upwards, and she saw me."

"Did you call the police?" I asked.

"That would have been the obvious thing to do, wouldn't it? But no, I didn't. I *froze.* I couldn't move. It was as if my entire body had been paralyzed. No matter how hard I tried, I just couldn't fucking move." He said, tears filling his blood-shot eyes.

"Moira was looking at me, pleading at me to help, but I just couldn't move. The men circled my wife and son, their gloved hands raised. One of them struck my wife in the face and hissed at her. This time I heard what he said."

"Give us the boy."

"My wife shook her head once more. She closed her eyes tightly. I cursed myself over and over. Why couldn't I do anything? What was wrong with me? My hand gripped the rail tightly, and I stared at it for the longest time, willing it to just fucking move, but it wouldn't budge." He said, looking at his frail, cancer ridden hands.

"Oh my god." I said without thinking, my hand covering my mouth.

He lifted his head and looked at me. His eyes were hollow, emotionless—as if someone had rammed novelty, prosthetic eyes into his bare sockets. They looked glassy, glazed over and oily. I couldn't maintain eye contact—this man terrified me, but I also felt pity, tremendous pity. He continued.

"All I could do was stand and watch as those *things* terrorised by wife and child. I tried to shout out, to scream, but no sound came out. It felt like my vocal cords had been bound with a tight rope. All I could manage was a croak. It was useless. I could do *nothing*. Can you imagine how that made me feel? I was convinced those men had something to do with it but that wasn't possible, right? It *couldn't* be possible, but nevertheless, there I was, rooted to the spot. I had no control."

"It felt like the ordeal lasted hours, but it couldn't have lasted more than 10 minutes. But the dread, the helplessness, the fucking endless terror I felt was so real. So *palpable*. They untied my son Troy as my wife fought against her restraints. I watched as my 12-year-old child pissed himself as they led him away. He screamed for his mother, for *me*. I watched as my son walked out of my life forever. I don't know how I knew, but I knew that I would never see him again."

"After they left, I felt some life come back into my body. I rushed to my wife and attempted to undo the robes that bound her but my hands, my fingers, they felt so fucking stiff! Eventually, the ropes came loose, and she was free. She screamed at me, clawed at my face. She was utterly inconsolable. It was all my fault. Why didn't I do anything? For God's sake, why didn't I fucking move?! I couldn't answer her. All I could say was that I was sorry, but what use was that? Who gives a fuck? Our son was gone, and it was all my fault."

"When the police arrived, we relayed the story. I told them how I had experienced temporary paralysis and that I couldn't explain it. They didn't believe me, and why would they? It was ridiculous. I could see the contempt in their eyes. It was the same way that Moira looked at me. I cried and pleaded with her, begged her to forgive me, to fucking *believe* me, but she wouldn't."

"Moira stayed with me a few weeks whilst the police carried out their investigation. They looked for our Troy, but they kept hitting dead end after dead end. It was a perfect abduction, they told us. Two weeks after the break in and Troy's abduction, Moira left me. I couldn't blame her. I couldn't live with myself either. After she left, I contemplated suicide, entertained the thought for some time before I decided against it. It wasn't long after that I had discovered the cancer, so I didn't have long, anyway. I decided to let the disease ravage me. And that brings us to... today."

For once in my life, I didn't know what to say. What could you say? In front of me lay a man, savaged by a debilitating disease, completely and utterly destroyed by his guilt. Not a single word that escaped my mouth would mean a thing to him. He was well past that.

"It wasn't your fault." Was all that I managed to utter. I regretted it instantly.

The black goo that surrounded Mr Rose intensified; it had started to *grow*. The thick sludge bubbled and oozed. I noticed the yellowish hue then, when the dim lights struck it—it resembled petroleum. It began to spill over the sides of the bed, leaking onto the dirt-stained floor. Without thinking, I moved my feet—I didn't want it to touch me. Mr Rose spoke again.

"Could you be a dear and get me a glass of water? I've not done that much talking for quite a while. My tonsils are on fire." He said.

"Of course, Mr Rose." I said and made my way into the kitchen.

When I returned to the room, the glass slipped from my moist palm and shattered on the wooden floor. I screamed out in fright.

"Mr Rose!!"

Allen Rose was completely submerged in the thick, black sludge—his body barely visible. I ran to his bed and, without thinking, plunged my hand deep into the substance. It felt warm, syrupy, and surprisingly smooth. I couldn't feel *him,* so I tried to take my hand out, but I couldn't. It was fucking stuck. I pulled and pulled with all the strength I could muster, but it was no use. My eyes widened when I saw tiny little hands emerge from the goo— hands that tried to *pull* me down further. I panicked, fear coursing through me like electricity. I didn't want to die.

I struggled with it for a few minutes before I was able to free myself.

I fell to the floor and looked up at the bed in awe. I saw something materialise from within—it was the body of a man. But whatever he was, he wasn't human. He stood tall and sinewy; his flesh nothing but oily, gooey matter. He looked like he'd been dipped in tar. He had no features—his face was nothing but a pulsing, warping mess. Fear twisted itself into knots in my stomach. I felt sick, on the verge of throwing up. I knew he had no eyes, but I could *feel* him watching me, looking at me. He opened his mouth and when he did, the slimy gunk squirted from within and fell to the floor in a clotted, mucousy puddle. He spoke.

"Guilt is tangible."

Then he melted; dissolved like a candle. I managed to get to my feet, wary of the bed facing me, but when I looked at it, I saw nothing but a drenched sheet. Allen Rose was gone.

***

I fucking ran. I ran as fast as my jellied legs would take me. I didn't know what to do, so I did… nothing. I told no one. What would I even tell them? Who would believe me? I knew that it was pointless. Katherine called me a few times. Work had called me relentlessly, but I switched my phone off and left town. I didn't want to be found. As selfish as it may sound, I just wanted to forget the whole thing. And I did… for a while.

Lately, I've realised that Allen Rose told me his story because he wanted me to believe him. He wanted me to *help* him but instead, I ran away. The guilt has been eating away at me these last few weeks. *Gnawing* at my insides.

Last night, I noticed something on my right hand—something black and sticky. It looked like oil or tar, and I couldn't rub it off.

The words that the man made of tar uttered to me reverberated in my skull as I watched the slick goo warp and throb on my hand.

"Guilt is tangible."

SLIT MOUTH GIRL

Her name was Clara, but everyone called her Slit Mouth Girl.

Bet you're wondering why, huh? I suppose it wouldn't be too hard to guess, though. Clara had a permanent smile, you see—a smile carved into her flesh by a jagged knife. It spread from cheek to cheek, almost touching her ears. The funny thing was, no one knew what happened to her. No one knew *who* gave her that perpetual smile. I don't think anyone wanted to know. I know I didn't.

Clara never spoke, never uttered a single word to anyone. She was like a grotesque version of The Joker. The crude stitching that adorned her cheeks would crack and splinter as her mouth quivered, then the blood would pour out in puddles and stain her pearly skin. The flesh around her mouth was permanently tarnished with this rusty hue—dried blood mixed with saliva and tears, I'd wager.

No one knew where she came from either—she just appeared in class one day. I remember the looks she got; repulsion mixed with fear. But she never batted an eyelid. It never seemed to bother her. Our teachers warned us not to make fun of her, warned us not to *leer,* but can you imagine how hard that was? It was impossible, but we all tried our best.

Children are cruel, though. Especially at an all-girl's school.

We made her life a literal, living hell. We'd sneer, we'd laugh, we'd point and say vicious things. Things I'd never thought I'd say. I wasn't a heartless person, but something about her made me detest her. I couldn't explain it.

Clara absorbed the abuse like a sponge—never once fighting back, never saying a word. Until one day… she did.

It was a day like any other. Clara sat alone on the playground bench, waiting and watching. Some of the kids surrounded her like a shrine and spouted abuse at her. I didn't join in that day.

She stood up and everyone fell silent. Her mouth opened as if she was going to speak, tearing the thick stitches that kept her face together—it came apart as seamlessly as laces on a corset. Blood leaked from her crudely torn flesh, forming a crimson pool on the concrete floor.

She opened her mouth *impossibly* wide and then she smiled. It was the most detestable smile I had ever seen in my life.

"You can come out now, Father."

Then her flesh came apart in pieces. It was like watching someone peel an onion. It crumbled like slices of warm meat, melting away almost. I stood with my heart in my mouth, watching this girl dissolve like liquid.

Inside stood a man, covered in blood and viscera. His skin was *glowing*, emanating this soft, warm hue.

"You have sinned, children. Now you will all be my vessels." He said.

"You will all be my Slit Mouth Girls."

MAGGIE THE MAGGOT

I used to know a girl called Maggie, we used to call her Maggie the Maggot. Why? You ask. You could probably hazard a guess that it had something to do with maggots, and you'd be right. Maggie the Maggot used to suffer from a condition called Myiasis; something she was born with, apparently. Poor Maggot Maggie used to just ooze maggot larvae, from every orifice of her body. They'd squirm and writhe in her eyes, crawling out and falling into her lunch. I couldn't imagine how many maggots poor Maggie consumed.

No one ever wanted to go near Maggie; they'd avoid her like the plague-ridden monster that she was. They'd give her odd looks when she walked past, leaving maggots in her trail. They'd hiss and sneer at her whilst stepping on her maggots, squishing them with their shoes. Maggie never deserved any of it. It wasn't her fault, after all.

I tried to befriend Maggie; I was the only one that didn't detest her for her maggot ridden ways—I even tried to befriend her maggots. I'd stroke them, let them wriggle in between my fingers; I'd even feed them. But after a while, the kids started to pick on me too and it wasn't something I wanted. Kids will be kids after all; they don't comprehend the effects their cruelty can have. So, I stopped talking to Maggie. I stopped caressing her maggots; instead, I joined in with the others.

I watched as they tormented her, holding her down and shoving her own maggots down her throat. Everything cruel that you can think of, they did to her. All the while, Maggie never said a word; never protested. Not once. Instead, I'd see her grinning ever so slightly. A smirk would envelop her face, and tiny little maggots would crawl out from the crevice of her lips. They'd slither around her mouth and occasionally, her tongue would pop out like a chameleon, and she'd eat them.

That was when I realised that Maggie the Maggot was planning something. Something… monumental.

On the day it happened, I was late to school; I had only just managed to make it in for the lunch hour. The afternoon seemed so painfully ordinary, so nondescript that the events that eventually unfolded now seem like a dream, a nightmare if you will.

I strolled into the canteen, and that was when I saw all the vomit. Within it, there were splatters of blood and squirming maggots. *So many maggots.* Bodies of my classmates lay strewn all over, their stomachs burst open at the seams; their insides decorated with sinewy viscera, the soft bodied larvae squirming and crawling.

Maggie the Maggot stood in the middle, a deranged, abhorrent smile spread across her larvae-stained lips, and she spoke.

"Now they are all like me."

WHEN THE LIGHTNING STRIKES...

They get closer.

***

Day 1

When the world ended, it wasn't like it is in the movies. People didn't scream or shout or run riot—nothing of the sort happened. We all just... accepted our fate. It was a quiet affair, to tell you the absolute truth—everyone just huddled at home with their families as they watched the sun burn out. Extinguish like a candle. It was there one minute and gone the next.

When darkness enveloped our world, no one knew what to do. It was just assumed the end of time was here, but we didn't know what waited for us in the darkness. We had no idea of the horrors that were yet to come.

Day 2

By day 2, the darkness was complete, impenetrable and flawless—pure black. I have never seen anything so utterly dark before. Even at night, you could still see stars, lights—your eyes would adjust, but when the world ended, there was nothing to see. We didn't know how we would survive at first—it was me and my wife.

We tried to make the best of it—not looking outside, just pretending that everything was as it was before. We still had electricity, at first anyway. So, we persevered, we fought with our urges to fall apart—we knew that if we let it happen, we would come apart at the seams. That was human nature, after all.

Day 7

On day 7, the thunder and lightning came. It was never ending. The constant ear-splitting rumble and the overwhelmingly bright flashes of light nearly blinded us. We didn't know what to do. We stood, snuggled together by the window, watching, waiting for… something. Anything.

Day 9

Day 9 was when we first saw them. They appeared with each bout of lightning and, with each flash, they were getting closer. There were 10 of them from what we could see outside our little house. They were grotesque, gnarly creatures; with elongated tendrils protruding out of every crevice of skin. They were terrifying.

Day 14

On day 14, we saw Graham Mills from next door outside. He was walking in a trance like fashion toward the creatures. His eyes had been burned from his skull. He was holding the limp body of his wife; blood trickled out of her mouth. Next to him walked a little boy.

They didn't have any children.

Day 20

"Daddy."

I heard a voice in the distance.

It's the voice of a little girl. I heard her as she walked up the stairs. Her meek footsteps echoed across the house. With each step, the thunder and lightning intensified. My wife stirred next to me and as she opened her eyes, I saw my own terror reflected in them.

"Daddy." It said softly, then it knocked on our door.

We didn't have a daughter.

MY DOG RUFUS

I've always preferred animals to people. You can commit to owning an animal safely knowing that you'll never get your feelings hurt, get abandoned or ever be judged. Humans are too flawed, too unpredictable, and I've had my heart fractured more times than I can count. I've lived alone for most of my adult life, something I guess others would find tragic and pathetic, but I've been *safe*. Safe from the despair I know many of you feel. That hasn't come without its flaws, though. I've suffered terrible loneliness. That all changed when I got Rufus though. He's been the only thing that's kept me going. Prevented me from dragging that knife across the bulbous veins on my wrists.

I was finally happy, something I've always lacked and yet craved desperately. He did that and no one else. Rufus was a rescue; purebred German Shepherd, and he was my best friend. No one ever looked at me the way that dog did. I was everything to him. It was so *pure*. So undeniably authentic, nothing else compared.

Sadly, a few years later, Rufus fell ill—cancer. It was terminal and there was nothing they could do. I was broken, completely devastated. It felt like being stabbed in the stomach, the blade submerging itself deep into my flesh, twisting and pulling. I was bleeding out, metaphorically of course, but that's what it felt like. Rufus was my life, and he was dying. I wanted to die with him.

I tried every treatment available and had Rufus pumped full of chemo. Nothing worked. With each passing day, he worsened. His once beautiful fur began to thin, fall out and he could barely move his skeletal frame. I'd have to clean up his piss and shit where he lay because he couldn't lift his brittle legs to carry himself out to the garden. It hurt me seeing him like this.

When Rufus began convulsing, that's when I knew I had to say goodbye. I could no longer sit and watch his eyes roll back into his head whilst his body trembled. I could no longer cradle his fragile, broken frame in my arms as he whimpered, confused. It was time. I didn't want to be cruel and keep him alive just for me; I had to let him go. I made the appointment at my local veterinary practice; they liked Rufus there so I knew they would be understanding, kind.

I sat in my car for the longest time, fucking crying like a baby and stroking his soft head. It used to fill me with immense comfort, but what I felt right there and then was dread. I was about to lose the only thing that ever mattered to me, and there was nothing I could do about it. I felt so helpless, so lost. I looked at Rufus, his eyes as white as milk, and I felt my heart fracture some more.

"It's ok, buddy. It'll be over soon." I said as I got out of the car.

With Rufus in my quivering arms, I walked over to the door and pressed the buzzer. I remember feeling like the whole world was closing in on me, clawing its way into my chest and squeezing tight. It was suffocating. I wasn't sure if I could do it, but I knew that I had to, for Rufus.

The receptionist saw my tear-stricken face and rushed to let me inside. Not a word passed between us. She knew why I was there. She'd seen this countless times. Weary owners with their blood-red eyes, the broken and the sick. There is a despair that perpetually permeates the air, utterly inescapable.

The waiting area was quiet, empty. I sat down and placed Rufus on the floor next to me; his chest moved awkwardly as I stroked him. He whimpered quietly, his strength waning. I put my face in my hands and tried to imagine my life without him. I couldn't. I decided right there and then that I was going to kill myself. I opened my eyes, feeling... relief? I guess that's what it was.

That was when I saw him, the man.

He looked misplaced, like he didn't belong there at all. He was dressed in the most immaculate suit I'd ever seen, coal black. He sat a few feet away from me, I didn't know how I hadn't noticed him before. He sat unmoving, staring straight ahead. There was something about him that unsettled me. He had this blank, void less stare that sent daggers through my heart. His eyes were the colour of grey chalk. On his lap was a tattered briefcase, elegantly placed. I tried my best not to look at him.

At that moment, I heard one of the consulting room doors open and I knew it was time. The vet called Rufus's name; my chest tightened as I stood up. My legs felt like jelly; wobbly and useless. I gathered Rufus in my arms and walked toward the person that was about to end his life and, subsequently, mine.

I lay Rufus on the glistening metallic table and kissed his little paw.

"Are you ready?" The vet asked me.

I looked up; my vision blurry. No, I wasn't ready.

"Yes." I said weakly. My voice sounded meek, not my own.

The vet picked up the catheter that was going to go into Rufus's paw. He gently shaved my boy's thin leg and inserted it. Rufus yelped as it went into his vein. I stroked him and whispered into his ear. I told him it was going to be okay, I wanted so desperately to believe it myself. I looked at the bottle of the Pentobarbital that stood on the table, the liquid death. The yellow solution warped and pulsated inside, making my stomach turn. This was it.

"He won't feel a thing", the vet's voice sounded far away, distant.

Rufus had no idea what was happening. All he knew was the pain he felt and even that he could barely comprehend—it was soul crushing. I just hoped that my being there, holding his paw and stroking his soft fur, would alleviate that confusion and pain somewhat. I think I was hoping that for my sake too.

"Here we go. You ready?"

I nodded, tears filling my eyes. I felt all the muscles in my body go rigid all at once. I watched as the vet's gloved hand began gently pushing the syringe. I watched as the bright yellow liquid flowed through the catheter, seeping inside my beloved Rufus. Death was instant.

***

When it was over, I decided that I desperately needed a drink—I yearned for something to numb the ache in my heart. I drove to a nearby bar, one that was close to my flat, as I knew there was no way I would be driving myself home. I drank until I couldn't see, until my vision was nothing but blurry movements and shadows. I was on the verge of passing out on the gunky table when I felt a tap on my shoulder.

"What ails you?" The voice said. I turned around to face whoever it was the voice belonged to. Ready to yell and scream at them to leave me the fuck alone.

It was a man. The same man that I saw at the vet's just a few hours ago. I tried to squint to see his face, but I couldn't. It was obscured by the dim lights. All I could see was his mouth, which was twisted into a detestable smile.

"My dog just died." I said.

"I can help you, you know." He said, his teeth gleamed in the feeble light.

"Help me how?" I asked.

"I can bring him back to life for you." He said, his smile stretching from ear to ear. There was something about his voice that I found grating; it was gruff, like someone had chiselled at his vocal chords with a sharp knife.

"Fuck you, you lunatic." I said and stood up to leave, but he gripped my arm. Tight.

"Isn't that what you want? I don't need anything in return, I simply want to help alleviate your pain." He whispered into my ear. I could smell his breath. It turned my stomach; I could feel the alcohol swishing around, threatening to escape. The scent lingered in the air—a mixture of stale whisky and something else… something rotten.

I freed myself from his herculean grip and stumbled out of the bar.

***

It hit me when I got home, the gravity of it all. My flat was so empty, so utterly lifeless, that I wasn't sure if I could get through the night alone. I collapsed on my bed, hoping for sleep to take me. Eventually, it did.

A faint scratching noise brought me back from my deep, drunken slumber. I remember waking up, momentarily unsure of where I was, of what happened. I looked for Rufus when it hit me, smashed into my mind like a tsunami, scrambling my thoughts. *He's dead, you stupid bitch.* That was when I heard it again, a faint but audible scraping at my front door; calcified nails on hardwood.

It was slow, yet desperate. I dragged myself from my bed, my head as heavy as lead.

As I approached, the scratching intensified, bellowing across my whole flat. I stumbled over to the front door; my vision blurred as I fumbled with the lock. When I opened it and saw what stood there, I threw up.

It was Rufus.

He stood on the carpeted landing, wagging his tail. I thought I was in some fucked dream, so I pinched my flesh tightly, the pain surging through my arm like an electric shock. No, this was real. I was awake. I remember thinking, *this is it*. I had finally snapped. My already fractured mind had cracked and crumbled amidst all this fucking misery. I was seeing shit. I must have been, because Rufus was dead, and I knew that. I watched him die.

And yet, here he was.

He scurried into my flat and placed himself on his bed. *As if nothing fucking happened.*

"What the fuck is going on." I managed to murmur, to myself, of course.

My chaotic mind drifted to the encounter I had a few hours before with the man in the suffocatingly trim suit. Was it possible? Could he have done this? The scent of his putrefying breath still lingered, smothering the air in my flat. It couldn't be true, could it? But Rufus *was* here, in the flesh. As real as you and me.

I gingerly tiptoed toward him. I had to feel him, had to see for myself. I crouched down and placed a shaky palm on his head. He felt *different*, somehow. His once soft fur felt coarse, like dry straw. Rufus looked up at me then and our eyes met. I suddenly felt naked, vulnerable. He had never looked at like this before, like he really *saw* me, you know? It was unsettling. I averted my gaze.

"Good boy." I managed to say before standing up.

This fatigue that I had never felt before suddenly washed over me like falling water. I staggered to my bed. Rufus observed my every movement, his eyes following me, darting back and forth. As soon as my head hit the pillow, I was asleep, but before I closed my eyes, I saw Rufus. For a moment, I could have sworn that he was *smiling*.

***

The next day, I woke up feeling like I'd been hit by a bus; my head was heavy, and my mouth screamed for water. The events from the previous day swirled in my mind like cigarette smoke. It all felt like a surreal dream, a very fucked up dream. Bred from trauma and severe intoxication. I needed a shower. I dragged myself from my bed and that was when I heard it, this detestable slurping noise.

It was coming from my kitchen.

My chest felt tight, as if gripped by a firm metallic hand. I tip-toed toward the noise, not daring to make a sound. I walked in and I saw him—Rufus. He stood by his barren food bowl, ears up and alert, *waiting.*

This was really happening.

He looked sheepish. Just how he used to look when he did something he shouldn't have, like pissing on the carpet or eating food out of the bins. My eyes widened when I saw what lay in front of him, the mutilated body of a cat. Its guts were splayed, maroon intestines lay scattered across the floor resembling thick, bulbous threadworms. A crimson lake surrounded its mangled body like lava.

My mouth was sour, bile rose in my throat, and I distinctly remember throwing up. Rufus looked up at me then and he smiled. He fucking *smiled,* I was sure of it this time. His teeth glistened brightly in the morning sun, saturated with blood.

I've read Stephen King's Pet Cemetery, you know. There was no fucking way I was letting that shit happen to me. I knew he came back wrong. I knew that this was not Rufus, and I knew what I had to do. I bashed his head in until it was nothing but a pulpy mess of sinewy tissue and I put his body in a black bag, along with the decayed corpse of the cat.

***

Later that night, I was still reeling from all that fucked up Pet Cemetery shit. It took me hours to clean up the blood. I sat on my floor in a haze, reliving everything. The grief of losing Rufus had somewhat waned, drifted away. I was worn out, so I had hoped that sleep would take me swiftly that night. Thankfully, it did.

It was the sound of panting that woke me up that time, the sound of heavy, laboured breathing. The first thing I saw when I opened my eyes was Rufus standing at the foot of my bed. He was covered in dirt and viscera; bits of serrated flesh hung limply to his snout as he breathed. He was back, but I couldn't understand how. Before I had the chance to fully absorb the lunacy that was encompassing me, I saw the blood. It shimmered in the dead of the night. There was *so much blood*. I whimpered when I saw who it belonged to. On my floor lay the corpse of a man. The butchered body of the vet, *my* vet. The one that put Rufus to sleep.

It was abhorrent. His flesh had been torn, shredded by a set of razor-sharp teeth. His lacerated torso was drenched in crimson, wet and glistening. He was missing all his fingers; I could see the exposed bone, the mangled skin.

This wasn't my fucking dog. Rufus was kind and gentle. The grief that I felt at his loss was still raw, tender like an open wound, and this travesty, this abomination, was trying to take his place. My mind raced. I felt on the verge of a nervous breakdown, but I willed myself to stay together; to not fall apart at the seams.

I was determined to make this thing disappear. I walked into my kitchen and retrieved the largest knife I could find. I decapitated not-Rufus, I carved into his unnatural, gooey flesh and cut him up into tiny little pieces. I drove for hours, buried the pieces of Rufus and the surgeon in a desolate forest just outside of town.

I prayed to God that it was over.

When I got home a short while later, I found Rufus sitting on my bed. He barked and growled at me; this guttural snarl escaped his blood-stained lips. He licked his teeth with this lacerated tongue and then he spoke.

"Wasn't this what you wanted?"

I think that was when something in me finally snapped.

Rufus was the only thing that had kept me going all these years and now he may be the one thing that will be the end of me.

***

I have tried to find the man responsible, the man with the impossibly trim suit and tattered briefcase. The man who did this to me. It has all been fruitless, though, utterly pointless. It was as if he never existed.

I have killed Rufus in every way imaginable. I have burned him, watched his flesh melt and sizzle until it was nothing but a gooey, flesh puddle. I have stabbed him, inserted the knife into every possible organ. I have cut off his head, again and again. I have even carved out his heart and yet, he returned.

I've killed my dog Rufus exactly 100 times now and he will not stop coming back. *Every single time.*

THE BOY WITH THE HALF-FINISHED FACE

The boy with the half-finished face—that's what they called him. He had a name, though; it was Marcus, and he was my friend. I first met Marcus when I was 14 and, despite his grotesque appearance, I liked him immediately. Once you got to know him, he was nice, timid; harmless really. Most importantly though, he was nice to me. My parents were killed the year prior, and I was bullied mercilessly for it. Marcus understood though—he sympathised with me because he didn't have any parents either. He had no one.

No one knew where he came from—he just appeared one day. With his half-finished face constantly oozing matter, he surprised us all. Repulsed us all to tell you the truth. When I first laid eyes on him, I had nightmares for days. It's quite difficult finding the words to describe Marcus's face, and I squirm at the thought of having to recall what he looked like. His face was misshapen, bulbous and bloated; like he'd been submerged in water for weeks.

All his features were stunted; like he'd not grown properly in the womb and came out an undeveloped foetus. His eyes were red raw slits; like they'd been cut open crudely with a butter knife. His nose was skeletal, puny and his nostrils were barely open. I used to wonder how he breathed properly. His mouth was the most terrifying thing of all; his bottom lip drooped awkwardly, like it wasn't quite attached, and his top lip didn't exist at all. It exposed all his gnarly, rotting teeth. He used to always ooze this liquid substance from his mouth, the colour of rust. No one ever knew what it was and none of us wanted to ask.

After a while, you got used to it though, you know I did anyway, and he became one of my best friends—for a while, at least. Until that *thing* happened on *that* horrible night. When Marcus did the unspeakable, when he did something I'd never thought he would do. But then, when do you ever truly *know* someone? For the longest time, I thought I knew him. I always sensed a darkness in him, though, a deep unfathomable wickedness that I guess came with having a half-finished face.

The night that it happened was like any other night. My foster parents were out, and I was in bed when I heard a creaking noise on the stairs; like someone was ascending very slowly. I got out of bed, and I opened my bedroom door slowly and that was when I saw that same, familiar rusty liquid.

Marcus was here.

I recoiled when I saw his face. It was... finished, complete. The thing that made me throw up, though, was the smell, the smell of a decayed corpse. Marcus's face was a mixture of my dead mum and my dead dad.

"I just wanted you to see your family again." He said.

PARANOIA

Doctor Murphy: What do you remember of the events from the last few days, Mr Ainsley?

Mr Ainsley: I remember everything, of course.

Doctor Murphy: Tell me what happened.

Mr Ainsley: The skinwalkers. They've been after me for years, wanting to use my flesh to complete their overthrow of our world. They've got nearly everyone so far. But I know, I can sniff them out like a dog searching for a bone.

Doctor Murphy: Please, go on.

Mr Ainsley: They take the flesh of a human being and wear it as their own. Others are unaware that they're in the presence of a skinwalker but I know, I'm not like everyone else, so I can discern the differences.

Doctor Murphy: What are the differences?

Mr Ainsley: They're so slight, so inconsequential that they can be quite hard to ascertain sometimes. But normally, you can tell by their gait and eyes. The key is in the eyes. Because they're not truly human, they don't quite know how to act like we do. Their walk is somewhat mechanical and stunted—like a toddler just learning to walk. But it's the eyes that give them away.

Doctor Murphy: What about the eyes?

Mr Ainsley: The eyes... they're vacant, but there is this eerie iridescent glow to them. The glassiness of them—they glimmer in the dim light and that's how you know. You can only tell if you stare at one for a long time and catch the reflection of the light.

Doctor Murphy: Tell me what happened last night, Mr Ainsley?

Mr Ainsley: One of them took over my mother.

Doctor Murphy: What did you do?

Mr Ainsley: There is only one thing you can do to kill a skinwalker.

Doctor Murphy: What's that?

Mr Ainsley: It's dirty work. You have to cut out the heart. Carve into the soft flesh, root around inside with your bare hands until you feel the bulbous lump. Their hearts are not like ours.

Doctor Murphy: Mr Ainsley, can I call you Todd? Skinwalkers don't exist. You are delusional. You carved out your own mother's heart and then ate it. You haven't been taking your medication.

Mr Ainsley: That's the funny thing about pills, Doc. They make your head all fuzzy and you don't see what's real.

Doctor Murphy: Not taking them also made you kill your mother.

Mr Ainsley: Oh Doctor Murphy, I didn't kill her. I did exactly what I was supposed to do.

Doctor Murphy: What do you mean?

Mr Ainsley: It got me here, Doc.

Doctor Murphy: Did you want to come here?

Mr Ainsley: Oooh yes. You see, Doctor Murphy, I needed to get here in order to initiate phase two of our plan.

Doctor Murphy: Your plan? What's your plan Mr Ainsley?

Mr Ainsley: I told you, didn't I?

Doctor Murphy: What's funny, Mr Ainsley?

Mr Ainsley: Oh that's right, I forgot. You still think I'm 'Mr Ainsley'. We are going to wear you real nice, Doc.

THE LOST CITY

When I decided to move to the countryside, I thought it would be the best thing for my mental health. I recently went through a bit of a sticky divorce—ex-wife got custody of the kids and somehow our mutually owned house. I was in a bad place for a long time; contemplated taking my own life—the whole shabang. I decided to see a therapist and, long story short, it was advised and eventually decided that I move away for a while—move somewhere quiet, empty and nondescript. The countryside would be the perfect place, right? At least I thought so anyway, at first.

I spent days scouring the housing market, looking for anything that would bring me a little bit of peace. Finally, I found a beautiful Victorian house in the next town over, a rustic little place. It was the description of the surrounding area and the house itself that really sold it for me. The small house was situated on the outskirts of an inviting and picturesque forest, nature galore. The house itself looked somewhat old but had a modern feel to it; weather worn white bricks that held old memories but could still manifest new ones. From the pictures, you could tell it had recently been painted. I was elated.

It took me a few days to gather and pack up the remaining few possessions that I had, and it wasn't long until I arrived at the new house. Now, I won't say that the house looked exactly like it did in the pictures, but they never really do, do they? It looked a bit more beat up upon closer inspection, and the whiteness of the place no longer had the same allure. The surrounding forest was overgrown and looked somewhat menacing—it looked suffocating; like if you'd walk in, the shabby leaves and lumbering trees would swallow you whole. In other words, it didn't look inviting.

I tried to kick the pesky thoughts away; I was here, and I was finally alone. That's basically what the doctor ordered, so I did my best to forget the strangeness of the place. Place it in the back of my mind like a soon to be forgotten memory. But I couldn't rid myself of the uneasy feeling that washed over me as I walked closer toward the house. I couldn't pinpoint what it was that made me feel that way either; it was like a persisting itch that you just couldn't scratch.

The inside of the house was a little different from the pictures, too, and not what I imagined it would be. Layers of dust covered every single nook and cranny; like it hadn't been touched by a duster for years. It was dark too, *too dark* for a summer's after-noon—it was as if the house itself devoured all the light that entered it. The furniture looked extremely dated—there were chairs, sofas and tables that I had never seen before. They were all shaped oddly too, crooked and warped. It didn't look like it belonged there, and it made me feel uncomfortable—*where did it come from?* I'd think to myself. I certainly wasn't going to keep it. I ended up throwing them out. I didn't realise then what a mistake that would be.

You shouldn't touch things that aren't yours.

I settled in quickly and focusing on myself was my priority—I wanted to get better with the hopes that I'd get to see my kids again. The first few days flew by with no incident—I read, took long walks, and was generally being a zen king. I started hearing the noises at the end of that first week. It was little things at first—things that could have been blamed on the fact that it was an old house. It's common knowledge that old houses just *exhume* strange sounds, right? Floorboards creaking, noisy pipes—that sort of thing. The strange thing was, the sounds that I was hearing seemed to be coming from *underneath* the house.

The sounds are quite hard to describe and, if I'm honest, quite mundane. Well, they were at first anyway. It was this intermittent scratching; as if someone was scraping long, calcified nails against hardwood. That's all it was. Every night at 2 or 3 in the morning, I'd hear it. It would last for an hour and then slowly cease. I tried to ignore it as best as I could—it didn't really bother me so much at first, anyway. After a while, it became just part of life. Unfortu-nately, it got worse—so much worse.

A few weeks later, I woke up one night, engulfed in sweat. I felt frightened and so utterly alone; the silence in the house was eerie and suffocating. It took me a few moments to recover, and that was when I started to hear the scratching again—only this time, it was accompanied by something else. It sounded like someone clicking their tongue; a horrible wet noise travelled up from underneath the house, reverberating off the walls in my room. The scratching grew louder and louder, to the point where I could bear it no longer.

I got out of bed and followed the sound, followed it all the way down into the basement. It was strongest here; almost filling the room. It was concentrated in one spot on the floor, which was covered by a carpet. With one brisk motion, I tossed the carpet aside and saw that underneath it was a boarded up wooden door.

I've watched enough horror films to know that you absolutely shouldn't investigate weird shit that you hear in your house, but in this instance, I was so *intrigued* by the door; drawn to it, I guess. I was desperate to find out what was behind it. Maybe it was the explorer in me or maybe I was just itching for something *different* to happen to me, something that would finally make me feel *alive*. Whatever it was, it made me pull up the boards on that door.

I stood outside the door for what felt like hours before I finally managed to pluck up the courage to open it. Cold, brisk air assaulted my face, followed by the foulest smell I had ever had the displeasure of inhaling in my whole life. My nostrils flared, and I had to stifle the chicken curry I had for my dinner that was threatening to come back up and decorate the basement floor. It's difficult to describe the stench—have you ever smelt gangrenous flesh? I have, and that's basically what it smelt like down there. This sweet, yet sharp smell emanated from within the opening. My eyes watered and I had to swallow the bile that travelled up my throat.

When the smell passed (or maybe I had just grown accustomed to it), I saw some stairs. You'd think after encountering the smell of literal death, I wouldn't even dream of taking a step further, but you're probably smarter than me. I was just too interested. A thought had occurred to me then—maybe that's why the place was so cheap, because the previous tenant was a homicidal maniac that had left some rotting corpses down there. Either way, I couldn't live with this shit and now that the rabbit hole had been unearthed, I had to explore it.

I descended the stairs and when I got to the bottom, I saw that I was in a stupendously large cave; it looked like some post-war underground facility. It was darker than dark down there, but I could see a faint glimmer of light up ahead. The curiosity within me took over the fear that was brewing, and I began walking toward the light. When I reached it, I realised that it was a torch—two torches, to be precise. They were placed on either side of a small, decrepit sign.

The City of Cardath

Now my first thoughts were generally a mixture of *what the fucks* and *this is impossibles*. It was the sort of sign that you'd see when entering small villages—wooden and hand painted. If you were entering a village in a fucking Grimm's fairy tale story. Everything about it looked old too. I stood staring at it, utterly stupefied. This had to be some sort of joke—there was no way that there was ever a city here.

I was torn away from my bizarre thoughts by a loud clicking of a tongue. I looked up and attempted to see into the darkness. The sounds were coming from deeper within the cave. I don't know why I continued further, but I did. I took one of the torches from above me and followed the sound.

As I walked deeper, I realised that I was in an actual city—large, derelict houses and buildings surrounded me. There was rubble everywhere, as if the city had been ravaged by war. It smelt of singed hair and burnt flesh and I could *feel* the sorrow that afflicted the place—echoes of the torment that occurred here pierced my heart. Everything looked ancient here, prehistoric even—the scorched buildings were not of the structure of modern times. They were incredibly tall to start with, but they protruded at impossible angles and if you looked at them for too long, the shape would warp and change. I averted my eyes and continued walking.

That was when I noticed all the strange symbols that were painted on each intact wall. It was an eye painted in a deep, menacing black with crimson arrows pointing in and out in various directions. I don't consider myself a deeply religious person, but you don't need to be to figure out that something occult happened there. The fear that had settled in the deep recesses of my stomach was threatening to engulf me like a rogue wave.

I couldn't take my eyes off the symbols but the same tongue clicking sound reached my ears once more, but this time, it sounded like it was coming from right behind me. I turned around and saw what I think was a deathly pale, veiny leg dashing behind one of the derelict houses. My blood turned to ice and I'm pretty sure my heart stopped beating right there and then. I held my breath and decided to get the fuck out—I didn't know what was down there and I sure as hell didn't want to stay and find out. I had seen enough.

I headed back the way I came, but that was when I noticed something different—there were people standing in the doorway of each building and house. At least, I thought they were people. They didn't look anything like you or me. They were impossibly tall with long gangly arms; their bodies were bulbous and cut up crudely. I realised then where the gangrene smell was coming from. Their skin was discoloured with shades of blue and purple, and I could see swollen purifying blisters full of brown fluid that had formed on their skin—many of which were oozing. They all stared at me; their eyes glowing like pale moons and what terrified me most was how ravenous each one of them looked.

One of them was holding a bundle of something small in its pus covered arms. It noticed that I was looking, and it extended its arms, and I vomited when I saw what was inside. I think it was a baby, but it was so deformed you could no longer tell. Its head was misshapen, like it had been gripped with a pair of forceps and forcefully pulled out of its mother's womb. Its eyes were little blood-filled slits, barely open, and it was sucking a blackened finger.

I found myself crying, I couldn't bear what I was seeing any longer. I needed to get out. I averted my eyes, and that was when I saw the gnarled fingers of those grotesque beings pointing at something behind me. I turned around slowly and saw a monstrous statue. At least I thought it was a statue until it... moved. It stirred and pulsated—like a heartbeat. It was adorned by torsos and various crimson coloured body parts. It opened its mouth, and these stifled grunts escaped—to which the people of Cardath responded with their own pained groans. Then they all opened their mouths, and I saw they had no tongues—all had been either ripped out or cut out.

I screamed. The human mind can only take so much before it finally crumbles, and I think mine was on the verge of disintegrating—it was as if a bomb was about to go off inside my head. I dropped the torch and ran; I ran as fast as my legs could take me. I was submerged in darkness, but at this point, I really didn't care—I just needed to get out of this bizarre and terrifying world. As I was running, I heard this piercing scream behind me and hundreds of feet hitting concrete—like they were all chasing me.

I think they were.

***

I managed to make it back to my basement—I boarded the door and put anything heavy that I could find on top. I wanted to keep whatever it was, inside. Occasionally, I heard pounding, scratching and a baby crying. I tried my best to ignore the sounds, but now that they'd seen there was a way out, I didn't know how long I'd be able to keep them all inside.

I didn't move out; I really couldn't tell you why. I think I felt responsible, somehow. I should have never opened that door and I should have never gone down there. I couldn't stop thinking about what I had found. The stench and sight of death was forever imprinted on my fragile mind. I was determined to find out as much as I could about the City of Cardath—I knew there was more at play here, more that could be unearthed. I had gone where no human being had ever gone before, and I could never go back from that.

One thing I did know, the people of Cardath were restless— they tasted freedom and they wanted out.

***

Living above a lost city certainly had its downsides and as soon as I discovered the City of Cardath, I had made it my mission to uncover what happened to its people. I frequented libraries, scoured old newspapers and combed the internet to find anything I could about the decimated city. As you can imagine, I had no luck. There was no information about the city *anywhere*. It was as if it never existed. Pretty soon, I started to doubt everything I saw there—maybe it was some sort of blip in my psyche, a momentary loss in cognitive function. Of course, I knew that it wasn't but either way, I tried my best to put it from my mind, but my obsession lingered like a bad smell and was only heightened every time I stepped foot in that treacherous basement.

The sounds. They never stopped.

I would hear them almost daily; the scratching and the tongue clicking would start in the night and would continue up until the very next morning. It drove me out of my mind. The things I saw down there haunted me as I slept; the mutilated bodies of the residents frequented my thoughts. The one thing that lingered and endured in my mind was one question. What happened to the people of Cardath? I needed to find out. But to find out, I would need to go back.

I had to put my expedition on hold when my ex-wife called to say that my son Noah was desperate to see me. He missed me, she said. He needed to see his father and whatever issues we were facing, we needed to put them aside in order to keep our children happy. There was no need to stir the hornet's nest, as they say, so I complied.

My son Noah arrived a few days later; elated to see me, of course, and we spent a few days enjoying each other's company. The City of Cardath was shifted to the back of my mind and for a while, I forgot all about it. The strange thing was, though, whilst my son was visiting, the sounds never once resurfaced. It was as if they *knew* I was no longer alone. To be honest, I was just happy to have a moment's peace. That's one thing I haven't been able to have ever since I moved down here, which was ironic really, when you think about it right? That was the whole reason I brought the wretched place.

One late evening, the night before Noah was due to go back to his mother's, we had decided to play a game of hide and seek. Noah was an inquisitive child and despite the small house, I knew he'd find a way to have fun with the game. Before we began, I took Noah aside and explicitly told him not to go in the basement.

"But why, Daddy?" He asked me, his little eyes welling up.

"Because the basement is no place for a little boy, Noah." I said, stroking his hair.

He nodded, albeit solemnly but I had hoped that my stern tone would deter him from going down there. Children are also notoriously afraid of basements, aren't they? My basement warranted that fear.

However, my son did what you would expect—he did the complete opposite. The house wasn't that big as I mentioned, so when I couldn't find Noah, panic rose in my throat like bile. My thoughts raced; crashing and tearing at each other like wild animals. I ran around the house like a loose cannon, throwing and crashing the furniture in my terror. I shouted for Noah; I screamed his name, but my worst fears were realised when I saw the basement door—it was open. A cold breeze licked at my bare feet. When I walked down there, I saw that the door into the abyss was open, too. I didn't know how he had managed to move everything I had placed on top—the furniture had been thrown aside.

I walked gingerly towards it—my throat dry and crackly, lacking moisture. I felt fear, but mixed in with that fear was anger. Why do kids never listen? I cursed Noah's inquisitive little mind. As I stepped foot into that dark, damp basement, all the memories of my encounter flooded back like a wave, and I found myself trembling like a lost puppy. I knew I would have to go inside and as that thought sunk in, I realised just how badly I didn't want to. But my son, Noah, I had to save him.

I followed the stairs down, just as I had before, and I was shrouded in darkness once more. I went toward the city—I felt as if my heart was being squeezed with a mighty hand. I faltered just outside the sign, the torches blaring with life; I wished then that their fire would somehow ignite some courage within me. I called his name, my voice meek and silent.

"Noah?"

There was no answer, just an overpowering and foreboding stillness.

I took a deep breath, lifted a torch, and proceeded on. A faint child's laugh reached my ears as I did so; I stopped to listen, but I could hear no more. The architecture of Cardath City surrounded me once more, the buildings and houses much the same as I had remembered them. I couldn't see any signs of life though, but I knew that they were there somewhere, hiding and biding their time.

Something seemed different, though; the deadness of the city and its people felt less absolute. The destitute I had felt before had faltered. As I searched for Noah, I saw a small fire and the silhouette of a man. Feeling hopeless, I approached him. As if sensing my presence, he whipped around, and I recoiled at the sight of him.

His skin was charred; ravaged by an inferno. He looked like he had literally climbed out of hell. One of his eyes was half closed, nothing but a slit—his other eye stared deep into my soul, and I had to avert my eyes. He wore nothing but ragged sheets over his frail frame; much of his exposed skin was covered in a plethora of infected blisters and pus-filled boils. I tried to feel pity, but the disgust I felt couldn't be concealed. The repugnant smell that permeated from this man is indescribable; a mixture of rotting flesh and dead tissue—that gangrenous smell I had described before.

He opened his mouth to speak, and I saw that his tongue was still intact, unlike the other residents of this devastated city.

"Who are you, and what are you doing here?" He asked. I felt almost accused.

"I-I'm looking for my son. Have you seen him?" I replied, my words failed me.

"There are many children here." He said, turning his gaze back to the blazing flames in front of him.

"He's a little boy. Blonde, green eyed. Doesn't belong here. Please, I have to find him," I said sternly.

"I have seen no such child." He spoke. "You shouldn't be here."

"He's here somewhere. He must be. Please, can you help me find him?" I asked, the terror that dogged my voice painfully apparent.

The man turned to look at me then.

"Do you want to know what happened here?"

Without thinking, I replied. "Yes."

"Then, sit." He said sternly.

I sat without complaint; something within me stirred—that same curiosity that first called me down here. As ashamed as I am to admit this, all thoughts of my son Noah faded to the back of my mind. I knew this wasn't me. I loved my son with all my heart. It was this place, this man. I was bewitched.

He began.

"Long ago, this city was prosperous. Its people full of life, full of dreams and hopes. The people of Cardath were simple, never yearning for much. We had crops, our population was growing steadily, and we weren't afflicted with diseases. Unlike the other cities that were around at the time."

"I guess we were just lucky." He said. "Or we were lucky until the Stranger came."

"The stranger?" I asked.

"He was a man from a different time, a different world to ours. Although we didn't know at the time, or maybe we just didn't care to know. With him, he brought death and destruction. He pillaged each person here. I was luckier than most, but you wouldn't think that by looking at me."

"What happened?" I asked.

"It was all my fault, really. Maybe that's why I was left somewhat unscathed, my tongue and own free will still intact. So that I can always remember what happened here. I am forced to look at my beloved city every day, forced to watch how it has warped and changed and forced to look at what my deeds have done to the people here."

"You see, when this Stranger came, he promised us things. Promised *me* things. I was mayor at the time, and I was greedy. The Stranger took advantage of that. He told me I could have everything I ever wanted. He said that our city and people will flourish. We just had to do a few things for would"

"What… things?" I asked. Out of the corner of my eye, I glimpsed the residents of Cardath city gathering. Clicking their teeth.

"He told us it wouldn't be much. All we had to do was accept his God. We weren't religious people, you understand. So, it wasn't difficult to accept some unknown God in order to help our city flourish. It was a small sacrifice, I had thought. I didn't know that it would destroy our whole city, I didn't know it would mean that my people had to suffer unimaginable torment. I didn't know."

"We prepared for the ritual the Stranger had set out for us. It was simple, really. We had to draw these symbols all over our buildings and then we had to build a fire and gather around it with the Stranger in the middle. When we were all prepared, the Stranger began chanting in a language that none of us had ever heard before—it was a most peculiar guttural noise. Like he was speaking with his throat. Do you know what I mean?"

I nodded, unable to speak.

"We were all so clueless, so utterly gullible. We smiled as the Stranger's body unravelled like a Christmas present. From within him rose the most mortifying creature. It declared with its many mouths that the city of Cardath was now his and we belonged to him. He then proceeded to tear everyone apart, women, children. Anyone and everyone. A lot of the residents didn't come out of fear, so a lot were hiding in their homes, but the Stranger found them and savaged them too."

"This city has been a wasteland ever since. It's people empty shells, feeding on themselves and each other. There is no humanity left here. Until you came along, of course." He smiled then.

"Now you have opened the door, you have shown them that there is a way out. More importantly, you have shown the Stranger that there are more souls, more cities for it to consume. You shouldn't have come down here."

He bared his teeth at me, and at that moment, I heard a scream. The scream of a child—my child. It was Noah.

***

The screams of Noah reverberated across the ravaged city; his anguished cries piercing my heart like a lead bullet. I looked around frantically, desperately trying to find him, but he was nowhere in sight. I looked back at the man, the Mayor and he too, had disappeared.

"Noah!" I screamed.

The residents of Cardath city had retreated back to whatever corner of hell they had derived from, and I was left completely alone. Alone and terrified; with terrible thoughts swirling around in my head. I saw Noah; his skin hanging off him like kebab meat— long, bloody strips of flesh dripping crimson. I saw Noah being devoured by the residents of Cardath with their charred hands deep inside his stomach, pulling out his intestines and then sucking on them like lollipop sticks.

The images that plagued my mind were unrelenting. I heard anguished cries coming at me from all directions; I could no longer tell who or what they belonged to. One thing I knew for certain, I had to find Noah and get out of there. I no longer cared about anything else, and I knew this city had to be destroyed; burnt to the ground, along with every macabre thing in it. As soon as I found Noah—I had to find Noah first.

I tried to go in the direction I thought the screams had derived from, but in a city completely adorned by rubble, it was hard to know which direction was the right one. I followed my gut none-theless and found myself back by the wall with the bizarre scrip-tures. The swirling patterns followed me as I made my way across; dirt sticking to my socks. I tried to be as quiet as I possibly could, as I had the overwhelming feeling that someone or something was watching me. I could feel eyes burning into the back of my head, but every time I turned around, there would be nothing there—just darkness and death. It was eerily silent; you could have heard a pin drop, should a pin have dropped anywhere. I felt uneasy; vulnerable.

I passed the scorched buildings in a blur. Everything was beginning to look the same and I couldn't discern where I was anymore; I felt like I had gone in circles. I knew I had walked for about two hours without encountering a single living (or dead) soul. I was beginning to lose hope that I'd ever find Noah when, out of the corner of my eye, I saw something. A small but bright fire; one that I was sure wasn't there before. I hobbled towards it, feeling the tiredness in my legs. As I got nearer, I noticed that fire wasn't a fire at all. It was a heart; a burning heart, and it was pulsating. As I got even closer, I saw that it was surrounded by something and as my eyes adjusted, I saw that it was a circle of bodies.

The bodies were strewn, but they had a kind of pattern to how they were laid out; each person lay contorted with their arms and legs twisted in directions I care not to describe, but curiously, they were all connected… by their fingers. A slight gracing of the fingertips is what tethered them together. It was a truly grotesque sight; seeing them all arranged like that. Their faces distorted; so twisted—it made me think of a wrung-out cloth. I didn't get any closer, but as if sensing my presence, the heart sprung to life— beating wildly.

I don't know what it was, but something drew me even closer and before I knew it, I was leaning over the heart—staring deep into its centre. I was hypnotised and enthralled by the swirling pattern; it seemed to almost move in a snakelike fashion. Slithering to and fro. Then suddenly, it ripped open to reveal a crimson-coloured eye. I jumped, falling backwards onto the bodies. The heart beat even faster, and the eye looked around frantically before fixing its gaze on me. The fire heart burned even brighter, and that was when I saw veins—veins that went deep into the earth like the tendrils of a jellyfish. I looked up, and I saw the ground—it lit up. The veins of this heart traversed the whole city.

Then the corpses began to stir. It was little things at first—a twitch of an eyelid, an unfurling of a lip. But it was noticeable— horrifyingly so. Then they all started to get up—their eyes were as white as milk and their mutilated bodies contorted robotically. They looked like deformed string puppets; their movements controlled by someone other than themselves. I stood, motionless; unable to move a muscle.

They all turned to look at me and I realised then that I was trapped; they encircled me.

I saw something behind one of their heads; it was a man, silhouetted by the darkness. As the light from the tendrils of the beating heart hit his face, I realised it was the Mayor. He was smiling.

"Please, help me." I said.

I examined him; he looked different to what he did only a mere few hours ago. His ragged clothing had been replaced; he now wore a long, black cloak that obscured most of his body. As I stared, dumbfounded, he opened it. Inside were thousands and thousands of little *maggots*. All swirling and writhing across his charred flesh, but they moved with a purpose; I could see that much. I saw that they were squirming over an outline of a small body, a child's body. *It was Noah.*

As soon as I saw my son's small, meagre body revealed, I tried to run to him, but the reanimated corpses of the residents blocked my path. One of them grabbed me by the arm; pulled it so hard that I thought it was going to be pulled out of its socket. I screamed. I fought. I kicked. I did everything I could to get myself away from them; to get to my son. Then I saw something glisten on the ground, a hammer. I don't know where it had come from, but I was certain it wasn't there before. I managed to free myself from their deathly grip, ducked down and picked up the hammer. Then I swung with all my might.

The first face I hit exploded—blood and viscera flew in all directions. I swung and swung, almost without looking, and was assaulted by a constant wave of blood. I ran toward the Mayor and Noah; I must have resembled a madman, but I didn't care. All I saw was red.

As I approached the Mayor and Noah; I saw hundreds of Cardath city residents approaching from either side. All were hungry for my son; all were reaching for him. Noah represented new life; a life they desperately yearned. He was a fledgling surrounded by predators that wanted to devour him, and I was running out of time to save him.

"It's no use. Your son is ours." The words of the Mayor sent a chill down my bruised spine.

"Let him go!" I shouted.

"His life will release us." Said the Mayor.

"It is time." He said, turning his gaze toward the residents.

I don't know what made me do what I did, but I turned around as fast as I could and ran back toward the circle. Toward the heart. With what strength I had left, I swung the hammer down on the heart, hard. I hit it until there was nothing left. Until it was nothing but a fleshy smear on the floor. The ground beneath me began to shake and as I turned to look behind me; I saw that the residents and, more importantly, the Mayor were all writhing on the floor. They screamed; blood flowed from their ears, eyes, and mouths.

I grabbed Noah, and I got the hell out of there. I ran and ran until I could no longer hear them. Once I reached the stairs back up into my basement; I heard something from deep within the cavern—a deep, guttural growl.

***

I moved out of that house the next day, but before I did, I made sure to seal the door to that hellish place using every single bit of wood I could find. I didn't want anyone else to go down there, didn't want anyone else to experience what I had experienced.

Noah had to have therapy after his encounter with Cardath City—he wouldn't speak, wouldn't sleep, and had terrible night terrors. My wife wouldn't let me see him and I struggled to explain everything that he and I saw; no one believed me. I miss him terribly and not a day goes by where I don't blame myself for what happened. If only I had left it well enough alone. Things wouldn't have turned out this way.

I live in a block of flats now; on the highest floor trying to forget the lost city of Cardath. Desperately wanting to forget the terrifying animalistic growl that I heard down there before Noah and I escaped. I don't know what it was, and I pray every day that I don't ever find out.

If you ever discover a lost city underneath your house, I beg you, don't go exploring.

FIRE

Doctor: Do you remember much about the fire?

Patient 1: I was in bed, I think. Then I was woken up by a stinging sensation in my nostrils. When I opened my eyes, I couldn't see anything. The smoke was overwhelming. As thick as fog.

Doctor: Then what happened?

Patient 1: My first instinct was to get to my sister. She was in the bed opposite to mine. The smoke was already filling my lungs; I could feel my chest tightening with a fiery grip. I could feel my eyes burning, overflowing with sooty tears. I pushed through, but my sister wasn't there.

Doctor: Where was she?

Patient 1: I didn't know at the time. I panicked and called for her, but all I could hear was the roar of the fire. She didn't answer me.

Doctor: And your parents?

Patient 1: I looked for them. They were in the room next to ours. As I fought my way through the smoke, I could already feel myself fading, so I knew I had to get out of there as fast as possible, but I couldn't leave without my sister. I couldn't find my parents either. Their door was ajar, but the room was empty.

Doctor: What did you do next?

Patient 1: That was when I heard the noise. It came from downstairs.

Doctor: It's okay, take your time.

Patient 1: I was groggy, on the verge of passing out, but I made my way downstairs. Followed the sound into the kitchen.

Doctor: What did you find there?

Patient 1: My sister. My parents.

Doctor: What were they doing?

Patient 1: My parents were dead. They weren't doing anything.

Doctor: And your sister?

Patient 1: She was sitting cross-legged on the floor, surrounded by blood. Her whole body looked like it had been bathed in crimson. She was smiling. The most detestable smile I had ever seen was spread across her bloodied face. She looked up when she saw me and then she spoke.

Doctor: What did she say?

Patient 1: *"We are free,"* she said.

Doctor: Free from what?

Patient 1: Free from our shackles, Doctor.

Doctor: What?

Patient 1: You see, I had forgotten who I was, but my sister never did. She knew who we were. Knew where we had come from and what we were capable of.

Doctor: And who are you?

Patient 1: Our parents, they tried to make us forget. To make us human like them, but they couldn't erase who we truly were. Children born of fire. And soon, the rest of the world will feel the touch of our flame.

Doctor: Your sister died in the house fire.

Patient 1: She didn't die, she was reborn. As was I. Can you smell that, doctor?

Doctor: W-w-hat's happening?!

Patient 1: Your reckoning.

HOARDER

Doctor's Notes

The patient is seen exhibiting symptoms of extreme hysteria and psychosis. The reason behind Tamara Tamechov's sudden dive into insanity is unknown. The below interview was my attempt to delve into her fractured mind.

***

Tamara: For the longest time, I thought my family was cursed.

Dr Pavlov: What makes you say that, Tamara?

Tamara: When everyone reached the age of 30, they disappeared. Never to be found again. I believed it was something that plagued our family name, something we would never be able to get rid of. My uncle John, auntie Flora, both my cousins Nancy and Dredd. My sister. All vanished without a trace.

Dr Pavlov: What did you think happened to them?

Tamara: I didn't know at first. I thought it was simply a coincidence when it happened to Uncle John and Auntie Flora, but when the rest started to vanish, I took it upon myself to find out what happened. Especially after my sister Toni. The police either couldn't or wouldn't do anything more to help.

Dr Pavlov: Do go on.

Tamara: I traced them to a family member I thought had been dead for years. My cousin Maya. She was a hoarder, you know. She lived in filth and squalor, surrounded by her own smut. It was disgusting. That's how I believed she died, drowning in it. I was wrong though.

Dr Pavlov: What made you think that this cousin had anything to do with the disappearances?

Tamara: Nothing at first. She was a recluse, a black sheep. No one in our family wanted anything to do with her. But after Toni disappeared, I had discovered that Maya had been sending letters begging for help. Pleading for help. The letters were quite pathetic. I decided to go down there.

Dr Pavlov: What did you discover when you got there?

Tamara: I saw and smelt the most unimaginable things. There were piles upon piles of boxes, cans, jugs filled with yellow liquid, packets of mould covered food. Everything disgusting that you could think of was all there.

Dr Pavlov: What happened next?

Tamara: The house was dark, and I couldn't see or hear much. I continued, fighting my way through the filth covered obstacles. I edged toward the only closed door in the house. As I got nearer, I heard a voice.

Dr Pavlov: Okay, go on.

Tamara: I opened the door, and that was when I saw them all. Uncle John, Auntie Flora, Nancy, Dredd and my poor sister Toni. She had them strung up crudely with metal wire. Their limbs were sewn on clumsily, disjointed. Their eyes were hollow, spooned out and their mutilated bodies were painted in an array of colours. Red liquid seeped out of every roughly re-joined wound. Maya stood by the corpse of my sister, carving out the flesh from around her mouth. Crafting an eternal smile. She looked around at me, her face manic, and she said, "Welcome to the Puppet Show."

THE BROKEN-DOWN TRAIN

Being an incident response manager on the London Underground can be a real drag. The constant need to be available can be a strain on your life, your relationships—the lot. My job title kind of speaks for itself—my main responsibility is to respond to, well...incidents and contain them as best as I can. Most of them are dull and repetitive. The 'incidents' that I have to deal with are train delays and those are always due to some drunk idiots. They are the main perpetrators. Another possible cause for delays is stray animals, an obstruction on the tracks and, you know, general train breakdowns. I won't bore you with the details.

I work specifically on the Metropolitan line, which is the oldest, most decrepit station in the city. It operates 24 hours Monday to Saturday and is one of the busiest stations in London. The station has been operational for decades, and that is evident in its crumbling brick and debilitating structure. It's a dark, cold and damp place that carries this aura of dread and uneasiness. Nothing creepy ever occurs there, but it's a hair-raising place, nonetheless. The perfect setting to a horror film. Well, nothing creepy ever occurred there until very recently and I have been struggling to comprehend exactly what it is that I saw and witnessed. I have never relayed the details of what happened the night my life changed, so in light of that, I would like to maintain complete anonymity so I will not divulge my name and where I live. Not that any of it would matter anyway—who I am is not important, but what I saw is.

The night the events occurred was beyond mundane and I wasn't even on site, but I was on call. At the time, I didn't live very far from the station. It was within walking distance so should anything immediate happen, I could be there quickly. It was a Thursday night, nearly the end of the week, and I sat in my flat, struggling to keep my eyes open. I drank coffee until I felt sick, but still, the fatigue persevered, and I desperately needed sleep. I glanced at my watch through blurry, sleep deprived eyes and saw that it was nearly 1am. If nothing has happened by now, then the rest of the night should be quiet and maybe I could get some much-needed rest.

I made another coffee and sat down and before I knew it, I drifted off.

I was awoken by a loud beeping noise and realised that it was my phone—an alert message. I fumbled for it, feeling groggy and disoriented. When I looked at the message, it made my heart sink. *"Urgh, I don't need this tonight. Bet it's another pisshead."* I thought to myself. The message was clear—something had happened, and I was needed urgently.

Feeling annoyed and frustrated, I threw on my coat and rushed out.

By the time I got there, the station was abandoned—a few late stragglers moved like zombies through the dimly lit station. I glanced at my alert message and the problem was at Platform 1—the westbound train. I made my way to the office—hoping to find some other colleagues that maybe could give me some indication of what the issue was. When I got to the office, though, I found it empty—not a soul in sight. I frowned, since this was a strange occurrence. There was *always* somebody here.

I began feeling a little anxious, and I wasn't sure why. Maybe they were out to lunch or went for a coffee. This wasn't a big deal. *"Calm yourself down,"* I told myself. I made my way to the platform and when I got there, I noticed just how eerily quiet and empty it was. I'd been on empty platforms plenty of times before. It's the nature of the job, but something about that night felt peculiar, like *something* wasn't quite right. I just didn't know what it was, not yet.

I saw the faint, dim lights of the train flicker up ahead in the darkened tunnel. I rolled my eyes at the sight of it, wondering what had happened this time to make it stop in the middle of the godforsaken tunnel. This is one of the aspects of my job that I detested the most—the train tracks were generally quite dangerous and, no matter your experience, things could still go wrong. I went toward the door that led into the tunnel whilst retrieving what I needed to get the job done—whatever the problem was. I couldn't see anything immediate upon first look—no obstructions on the track. It looked like it had just stopped. Everything appeared to be functional. I would have to get on board and speak with the driver.

I walked toward the front of the train, observing the interior on my way. The inside of the train was in complete darkness—as if all the light had been plucked from within. It was pitch black. *"What the hell?"* I wondered to myself. This was incredibly unusual. The train hadn't lost any power because I could still hear the engine grunting and moaning. The only logical explanation I could think of was that maybe the bulbs blew inside the carriages, but I'd *never* seen that happen. *"Just because it has never happened doesn't mean that it never could."* I reasoned with myself. I reached the driver booth and peered in, noticing that it was empty.

What the fuck.

A driver was never permitted to leave his post with the engine still running—it risked lives unnecessarily. I felt the fear I was feeling dwindle within me and it was then replaced with anger and annoyance. I was ready to give this driver a piece of my mind when I located him. I tried the door, and it was unlocked. Another transgression. I walked in gingerly—it was so dark inside. I retrieved my flashlight and fumbled with the controls. Everything seemed to be in working order, nothing broken—nothing that would have caused whatever was happening here.

Then I heard something. A soft, yet anguished wail. I nearly jumped out of my skin. The sound came from behind me—in the train carriages beyond the door. I had never felt fear like this before—it was entirely alien to me and I wasn't sure how to handle it. I considered myself an extremely level-headed and logical person. I didn't fear the dark, but I guess I feared the *unknown.* Doesn't everyone? Whatever was happening here, I didn't know how to handle it. My brain couldn't compute with the unknown.

I braced myself to walk through the door—I didn't know what I was going to find beyond, so I knew that I needed to be prepared. The rational side of my brain was working hard to vindicate the irrational thoughts that seemed to be seeping into my mind like spilled wine on carpet.

When I walked in, I couldn't see anything and, with a quivering hand, lifted my flashlight. At that moment, all the lights in the carriage turned on.

I was not prepared for what I saw.

All the passengers were there. They were all standing in a perfect line facing the wall. I couldn't see any of their faces—they were all obscured by one another. They stood so close, *too* close. I stared, flabbergasted. *What was happening here?!* I couldn't move, I didn't dare. I was paralysed to the spot.

"Hello?" I said, my voice quivered as I spoke.

No one answered.

They all stood eerily still. You know how the human body always makes *some* sort of movement? The rising of the chest as you exhale or inhale. The sudden, yet minor involuntary jerks of the body in its natural state. Do you know what I'm talking about? You must. Well, these people, they were completely stationary. There was *nothing.* Absolutely nothing, and it terrified me.

I managed to move my body, to walk closer, but I couldn't tear my eyes away from them. What were they doing? Was this some sort of joke? A mutual prank? I slowly reached into my pocket to retrieve my mobile phone—I had to call someone. Then I realised that I was underground and there was no service down here. I cursed under my breath.

That was when I heard that soft, yet anguished wail, again. It came from further down the row of these human statues. I strained my neck and saw that it was the driver—he had the TFL uniform on. My body regained its fervour, and I ran toward him, panting heavily.

"Hey, what's going on?" I said to him. He, too, was facing the wall like the others, but his body was at least *moving.* Jerking in awkward motions.

His shoulders quivered and shook—that was when I realised that he was crying softly.

"Mate, are you ok?" I asked again.

He didn't answer, but began to slowly turn toward me. When I saw his face, my heart nearly leaped out of my mouth.

His eyes were missing. I looked deep into his barren, blood caked holes and I cried out. I could see the congealed blood, the crust that caked the skin beneath. He looked at me, really *looked* like he could see me. Even though his eyes had been plucked from within his head.

"Help me, please." He said.

"What can I do? What happened to you?" I replied.

"It's them. They're coming. Please."

"What happened er… Tony? Is that your name? Who's coming?" I asked.

"Oh god, they're already here. You don't understand. They take YOUR EYES. That's how they get to your soul!" He screamed.

Before I could say anything further, he turned away, but it was almost like he didn't turn away voluntarily. It was as if someone forced him to face the wall. Like there were invisible hands enveloping his body, making him do their bidding.

At that moment, every single person in the carriage arched their backs. I heard their bones snap and crack like fragile branches of a derelict tree. I saw that none of them had eyes—just empty, crimson-coloured sockets. Then they opened their mouths—wider than I thought was humanly possible. *It wasn't possible.* Then I watched as their throats constricted and morphed, like something was inside—trying to crawl out. I began backing away, looking for any other possible exit. I couldn't see one.

I heard a screeching sound and whipped around, sweat pouring off me in buckets. One of the train doors had opened. Something large and wet smacked the ground, mimicking the sound of meat hitting a slab. Then, whatever it was, it slithered further into the carriage. I thought I was going to vomit out my insides when I saw the disgusting thing. I don't know what it was, but I was certain that it wasn't human. It made sloppy, slurping noises as it slid further and further into the train. A wet, blubbering puddle of matter lay in front of me. It looked like a moving, living lump of jelly—sticky and moist. It had no body, not a solid body anyway, but its eyes were piercing—*human*. It dawned on me then, where those eyes came from.

It looked at me and formed what I think was a smile. A detestable smile that dribbled and contorted. I screamed then. I didn't know what else to do. It continued to move its grotesque, limp and gelatine-like form toward me. I had to get out of there.

I turned around and saw that every passenger was gone. *Vanished.* Then I noticed that each train carriage door was open, and I could hear that squelching noise all around me. They were coming.

I ran toward the driver door—ran as fast as my legs could take me. When I exited the train, I looked behind me and really wished I hadn't. They were all slithering toward me, and they were moving *fast*. I continued running until I was back on the platform, until I was out of that godforsaken station.

I limped home.

***

I thought about going back to work the next day, but I just couldn't. I couldn't face it. I knew that no one would believe me, knew that I would be dubbed a crazy person and I couldn't handle that. I *know* what I saw, but it was impossible to form into any kind of logical explanation and that was because what I saw was anything but logical.

I looked for a guy called Tony—asked around and learned that Tony went missing the day before that night, along with 15 other passengers. No one could explain it. No one even *wanted* to. A colleague tried to let me know before my shift but claimed that his messages wouldn't go through. I didn't understand. I quit my job after that.

No one ever reported a broken-down train on the Metropolitan line that night and I'll never understand what I experienced or what happened to those people but one thing I do know, I'll never forget those wet, slurping sounds I heard that, and I'll never forget how that rippling mess of a creature smiled at me.

THE COFFIN

When the coffin first appeared on the night service of the Jubilee line, I was the first to discover it. It was the most bizarre and yet innocuous thing. It looked like it belonged there, but it absolutely didn't. It stood, leaning against the door, the bright fluorescent lights bounced off it like rays of the sun. It was a deep, dark brown; made of oakwood. There was not a single scratch on it, it was brand new and without blemishes.

I found it whilst I was performing my nightly cleaning duties—I used to work on the London Underground. My job consisted of many things, but essentially my forte was the Lost and Found. A dull, thankless and uninspiring job but it paid the bills, so I rarely complained. I had a daughter to support, after all.

I radioed my colleague Jason, who was just as confused and creeped out as I was.

"What do we do with it?" He asked.

"Well, it can't stay here. We're going to have to move it to the lost and found." I replied, feeling a little foolish.

"Who the fuck loses a *coffin??*" He asked.

I didn't have a reply. What could I say? He was right, who in the world misplaces a coffin? It just doesn't happen. Yet here we were, staring the impossible in the face.

"Come on, we've gotta move it." I said, tugging Jason's torn sleeve.

As we neared, the air suddenly thickened. Akin to the sudden change in climate as you step off a plane in a hot country. It was suffocating. I turned to look at Jason and saw the sweat forming on his brow. He felt it too. I placed a sweaty palm on the surface of the coffin, and it chilled my skin, it was so cold. When we eventually lifted it, it was as light as a feather—indicating to us both that it was indeed empty. Had to be.

We carried it all the way to the lost and found booth in total silence. Neither of us spoke; we felt like we couldn't. As if speaking out of turn would serve as disrespect to the dead. It was silly, I know, but we felt *compelled*. At least I know I did.

Not knowing what else to do, we left the coffin inside a disused closet, and that's where it stayed. Until the next morning, at least.

***

When I arrived at work the very next day, I found Jason in the lost and found booth, his face as pale as the moon.

"What happened?" I asked.

He looked up at me, eyes all glassy and watery.

"Something... happened." He said softly.

"What?! What the fuck happened, Jason?"

"They found something weird on the tube last night, man." He said, not taking his eyes off the closet where we left the coffin.

"Weird how? What do you mean?" I asked. He was starting to annoy me, being all cryptic.

"There was so *much* blood. It was everywhere. It covered the walls, the floor, the seats." He said, I could hear the fear that dogged his voice.

"Jesus. What was it? Suicide?"

"Without a body?" He asked.

He was right, of course.

"There is something else." Jason said, glancing at the closet door.

"What?" I asked.

"The coffin is gone."

When I walked over and opened the closet door, I saw that the coffin was no longer inside. We checked the cameras, and no one went in and out of the Lost and Found that night. It was as if the coffin vanished into thin air, it wasn't possible, of course, but it happened. It was gone.

That day went by in a blur—we had police crowding the station and the aforementioned train. Everyone was left with more questions than answers, including the police. They interviewed me and Jason. We weren't even on shift that night, so there wasn't a lot we could say, nothing we could help with. We didn't mention the coffin though, we didn't think anyone would believe us and why would they? The events were perplexing enough as it is, and we didn't want to add more fuel to the already roaring fire. What was the point? The coffin was gone, and I just wanted to forget about it.

Jason and I worked the rest of that day in total silence. Not a single word passed between us. I guess the utter ridiculousness of everything that occurred in the last 24 hours really got under our skin. I couldn't stop thinking about the coffin. Why was it there? Who put it there? What did it mean? It was eerie, and it burrowed deep into my heart like an earthworm. I also feared it. Everyone fears coffins though, don't they? I guess it's because they represent death and, as humans, we all fear its eventual grasp on us all. Was I experiencing some sort of moral dilemma? I wasn't sure. Death is something I seldom understood and not something I've had first-hand experience with.

Not until I discovered that coffin for the second time.

It was a few days after the first encounter—I was working the night shift that night. I was alone. Jason hadn't shown up for work that morning. I tried to call him, but he wouldn't answer his phone. I was worried, but I didn't know why. *He's fine, just sick*, I told myself.

I got onto the westbound Jubilee train, black backpack in tow, and that was when I saw it again. Its obtrusive presence suffocating the small carriage. It was so much bigger than I remembered it. I was cautious as I approached it, wary of any sudden movements I made. I don't know why; I honestly can't say why I felt so terrified. I guess that's how you react when you are faced with something unexplainable. What the fuck was it doing here again?

I got the sudden urge to open it. This feeling of overwhelming need washed over me as I stood inches from its glistening oakwood finish. My trembling hand reached out, as if not my own, and touched the smooth exterior. I felt a vibration underneath my moistened fingertips, as if something quivered within. *Something was inside.*

I opened the coffin and peered inside. What I saw almost made my heart leap out of my chest.

Within the casket, I saw blood. *So much blood.* As my eyes adjusted, I saw bits of jagged flesh hanging limply inside, as if cut by a serrated blade. Peering in closer, it looked like the coffin was bottomless and all I could see looking inside was pure darkness. I retrieved a torch and hesitantly flicked the switch. There were bloodied chains and stained hooks, one of which had a disembodied, rotten human arm attached to it. Body parts lay strewn across the soiled bottom of the coffin, and I gagged as the smell travelled up my nostrils. It was a sweet and yet sickly scent—the smell of meat under a hot sun.

As I backed away, that was when I saw something else that caught my eye. It was a lanyard and attached to it was an access card. An access card that only an employee would have. My blood chilled in my veins as I saw the name that was written on its blood-soaked surface.

Jason Brown

I got the fuck out of there then—rushed to get someone, anyone who could help. I called the police and waited anxiously. I tried Jason again multiple times, but his phone was dead—all I could hear was static.

When the police arrived at the scene that night, all traces of the coffin had been erased—it had vanished once more. Everyone deemed me to be a time waster, an idle lunatic. I know what I saw though—the images had been imprinted on the insides of my retinas and it's something I would never forget. The coffin made sure I wouldn't forget.

Jason was never found.

***

Tonight was my last shift. I couldn't do it anymore, so I quit. Seeing what I saw had taken its toll on my somewhat fractured brain. For my last shift, I refused to work the westbound Jubilee train, as I knew what would be waiting for me, if I did.

I was cleaning out one of the Northern Line carriages when my phone pinged. It was from my daughter, Tracey.

Hey Dad!

I'm just on the westbound Jubilee train, the last train of the night. I've got reception for a bit so thought I'd send you a text, so you don't worry. Hoping you'll get this before I cut out again.

It's a little eerie! The train is empty apart from me, but I can see something tall and brown in one of the further carriages. I hate being in these carriages alone so late.

See you soon! Love you.

Tracey never made it off that train.

PORRIDGE

Porridge... am I right?

I detested it as a kid. Perhaps it was the sticky, syrupy texture and how awful it felt as it travelled down my throat, enveloping my tonsils, making me feel like I was about to choke. Maybe it was its bland taste. Either way, it was rancid.

My mother used to force me to eat it—every fucking morning without fail.

"Eat your porridge, Benjamin!" She'd squeal.

If I refused, she would hold my nose until I couldn't breathe and then shove the disgusting gooey stuff down my unsuspecting throat. She really was a wicked woman—she relished in the suffering and misfortune of others. When little Patrick from next door fell off his bike and twisted his ankle, I watched my mother's mouth quiver—forming a smirk. It delighted her.

As time went on, my mother became withdrawn. She was moody, barely venturing out of her bedroom. Except for when she had to feed me porridge. That was the only time I saw her. I didn't like how she looked at me, though—there was this sparkle in her eye as she watched me lift the spoon into my mouth. *Like she knew something that I didn't.* She'd watch me spoon the detestable goo into my mouth and a victorious smile would spread across her face. As if she'd won a battle.

I guess... she did. I just didn't know at the time.

Pretty soon my porridge started tasting different, too. It was somehow *worse* than before. Instead of the usual bland taste, my taste buds were assaulted by this sourness that I couldn't describe. It tasted spoilt. When I broached the subject with my mother, her face would turn as sour as the porridge that I was eating.

"Benjamin! I am sick and tired of your excuses!" She'd hiss at me.

Things only proved to escalate. The taste of the porridge grew more rancid and viler with each passing day. My mother became more and more manic. Her hair was a bird's nest that fell in awful, straw-like strands about her hunched shoulders. Her face was gaunt, pale and her under eyes looked heavy, discoloured like old tea bags. Her smile never wavered, though. As soon as she put that detestable mucus in front of me, her mouth would quiver.

One morning, I woke up to find our kitchen empty. No sign of my mother. I went toward her bedroom and noticed that the door was slightly ajar. As I walked in, this rancid, putrid smell hit me in the face like a brick. It was emanating from the bathroom.

When I walked in, I almost fainted.

My mother was elbow deep in the chest cavity of little Patrick—her arms saturated by rotten flesh and putrid tissue; all sticky and glossy. I peeked inside and saw the gooey, soupy mess that was Patrick.

It looked exactly like my porridge.

"Are you ready for breakfast, Benjamin?" My mother asked, smiling.

COCKROACH BOY

My son Vernon was always quite odd. One of his favourite pastimes was keeping insects, mainly cockroaches. As a mother, of course I was concerned as it wasn't the sort of thing that a child should have been occupying himself with, so I tried my best to discourage and foil the obsession, but there is only so much one can do.

I didn't want my child to grow up hating me, so eventually, I relented, and I let him continue pursuing his fixation—under close eye, of course. I thought it was nothing but a fad, a whim and something that would eventually right itself. Children are quite fickle, unpredictable. So, you know, I wasn't *overly* apprehensive, not at first.

He would collect any insect he could find—his favourite thing was frequenting nearby woodland areas and parks, rummaging around in the damp earth to see what creepy crawly he could fish out. He even went as far as to beg me to buy him a lizard so that he could always have various insects to stare and ogle at around the house. I caved and bought him a bearded dragon who he named Rosie. Bearded dragons devour all sorts of insects and roaches were one of the main delicacies. I wasn't a fan, but it made Vernon happy, and what else could a mother want? After a while, he started breeding them to make his own colony. *"Some for Rosie and some for me, mummy!"* He used to say.

Our spare bedroom was full to the brim with containers of various sizes—all encasing these nasty little creatures. Vernon would spend hours tending to them. I'd walk in and find him elbow deep inside the mountain of roaches—the creatures scuttled up and down his little arms. He'd sit there, his face a picture of happiness.

He'd be there for hours, eyes closed and smiling. I'd always wondered what he was thinking about—what was going through his little mind as he sat there.

I had a weird little kid.

I had my limits, though. I forbade Vernon from having them in his room or any other place in the house. They were to be confined to one space and nowhere else. For a while, Vernon listened. He was okay with it, and it didn't bother him. But I noticed that he wanted to leave our spare bedroom less and less. Refusing to go to bed when I asked him to, often demanding that I let him sleep in the spare room with Rosie and his beloved roaches.

I said no, of course, but every time I did, I could feel his little eyes darting toward me like daggers—I didn't like how he looked at me.

"I thought you were a good mummy." He'd say to me.

I'd frown. His words stung, and I think he knew that.

"I am a good mummy, Vernon." I'd say, wrapping my arms around him.

He'd wriggle out from under my embrace. The anger would just radiate off him.

"I wish my mummy was roaches." He'd say.

During times like this, being a single mother was difficult, and I yearned for Vernon's father, Cecil, to be around more. He only came at weekends and with each visit, Vernon would distance himself more and more.

Cecil wasn't too pleased with the fact that I was letting Vernon play around with insects but in fairness to me, I was doing my best and if he wanted to raise his child his own way, then he shouldn't have abandoned us for that slut Victoria. I told him as much.

As time went on, Vernon became increasingly more consumed by his addiction. He started to disobey me and one morning I found his room covered with jars, buckets, a plethora of different sized containers; all filled with these slimy, winged creatures. It was disgusting as well as disturbing, but I was at a loss for what to do. I demanded Vernon dispose of them. He would look at me with a terrifyingly vacant expression and outright refuse.

"No, Agatha." He'd say.

Agatha? He's never called me that before.

"I am your mother, Vernon, and you will do as I say! Now you get rid of these things at once!"

I'd had enough by this point.

The next day, as if by miracle, there would be double the amount of the squirming things. I couldn't fathom how they were multiplying so quickly.

I had noticed other changes within Vernon. He was becoming more withdrawn, quiet and aloof. Basically, it wasn't the sort of behaviour that a 10-year-old should be exhibiting. I started hearing peculiar sounds emanating from within his room too, sounds of chewing, crunching. When I'd take a peek, I'd see Vernon lowering one of the roaches into his mouth. They would wriggle and protest, but Vernon would shut down their complaints by a loud and hard smack of his little teeth. He'd sit and chew for a long time before he finally swallowed, and my flesh would be assaulted by goosebumps watching him. I had decided that enough was enough when I watched him put his hand down his throat and retrieve a spiked leg.

A few nights later, I was in bed. My deep sleep was interrupted by sounds of scratching. As I suspected, the noises were coming from within Vernon's room. I was apprehensive when I approached it. I really didn't know why. Something at the back of my mind was telling me not to.

When I entered, the room was pitch black, and I fumbled for the light switch. When I flicked it on, the sight that assaulted my eyes was unspeakable. Roaches filled every crevice of the room, every little hole—they were everywhere. They squirmed and scurried all over each other. Vernon was leaning over Cecil, his father. I watched as my husband's stomach constricted, morphed and quivered. Then the skin ripped open, splitting at the fleshy seams. It tore apart as easily as a sheet of paper. Inside, a million cockroaches slithered and thrashed.

"Vernon, what have you done?" I screamed.

Vernon beamed happily, a crazed grin from chin to chin. *"Daddy is roaches now, mummy!"*

***

I only get to visit my son on weekends now. He resides in a psychiatric facility just outside of town. He is more withdrawn than ever—hasn't spoken since that night. I blame myself more and more each day, wishing that I'd done something, anything. I should have never let it get that far. I just wanted Vernon to be happy. Isn't that what every parent wants for their child? Endless happiness? I made a mistake that will haunt me until the end of my days. Everyone makes mistakes, don't they? We're not all picture-perfect parents and I was trying my best.

Was Cecil's death my fault? Yes, I wholeheartedly believe that it was, and I will spend the rest of my life atoning for that. Was how Vernon turned out my fault? I don't know. I don't think I'll ever know.

I rid my house of the cockroaches, flushed them all down the fucking toilet—every single one. I had to rehome the lizard because I couldn't bring myself to feed it what it needed. I have tried to make some sort of life for myself since the incident, but how can you truly forget something like that? I lost my child. I lost his father. It was difficult.

I've been having trouble sleeping lately. I keep having nightmares. I can't rid the image of Cecil laying there, his stomach ripped open, cockroaches all writhing and squirming inside. It's haunting. I think I've been *hearing* things recently too—strange scratching sounds. They have been coming from Vernon's bedroom. I haven't been able to go in his room since it all happened, but who can blame me?

I finally did the other night. I haven't been able to explain what I saw inside.

When I walked into his room, I saw a small pile of cockroaches on the floor—squirming and wriggling. As I neared, they started shifting and morphing. *Forming words.*

"You shouldn't have done that, mummy."

THE BIRTHDAY GIFT

I received the first package on the morning of my birthday. I was cautious. No one was supposed to know this address. How could this be? My heart quivered inside my chest as I picked up the package. *He* can't possibly know I'm here. I was so careful.

I examined the small, rectangular box that was revealed to be inside. Written on the top was—*From your secret admirer*. I found myself short of breath. Who could this be? I thought about just discarding it, throwing it away, but something within me compelled me to open it.

What I saw inside nauseated my stomach.

Wrapped in a bunch of decayed roses, was a freshly severed human finger. It was crudely cut off; I could see the jagged edge skin that surrounded the amputated bone. It smelt putrid though, like rotten flesh. Dried blood tainted the interior of the box.

Before I had a chance to react, I felt this searing pain in my right hand. It was as if all the synapses in my brain lit up at once, like a firework had been set off inside my mind. Once the pain had depleted somewhat, I looked down at my right hand. I nearly passed out when I saw that my index finger had disappeared. *Simply fucking vanished*. I panicked. I screamed until I couldn't breathe. It looked like my finger had been severed—*cut off*.

Then I heard a knock on my door. I rushed to open it. I found another box—it was in the shape of a dog bone. Inside, wrapped in crimson-coloured vines, was a coarsely hacked off rib—perfectly cleaned. The bone glistened as I stared at it. Then suddenly, I was overwhelmed by this roaring pain in my left side—as if someone had their hands wrapped around my lungs, squeezing them tight. I found myself unable to breathe. *I felt something snap inside*.

Who was doing this to me?

I received 4 more 'presents' like that—each contained a rib, a kidney and a left eyeball. You could hazard a guess what happened after I opened them. Each box was the size and shape of the organ that I was going to lose. I was foolish, I know that. I should have left the boxes well enough alone and called the police, but I just couldn't. Something within me prevented me from doing so. I was now missing a rib, a kidney, and my left eyeball. Not to mention my index finger.

There was one more package waiting for me outside my door. I don't know how I knew it was there, I just knew. *My final present.*

This one was in the shape of a heart and there was a note.

You promised me every piece of you, Jane. You vowed to be mine until death us do part. You promised me your heart. You never should have left me.

Happy Birthday.

HER NAME IS ANNA

Entry 1

I am a mother.

Her name is Anna, and she was the most beautiful thing. Yes, I know that's something that all parents say. But it was true, she was. She glowed—there was no other way to describe it. It was like looking at the sun. Otherworldly.

I never remembered her father—guess that was the conse-quence of a drunken one-night stand, but the curious thing was, I remembered nothing of that night. It was like an itch that I couldn't scratch. A misplaced, missing memory that I longed for like a new-born cub longs for its mother's teat. But when I'd try to piece it together like a puzzle—Anna would cry for me, and I would care about nothing else.

Entry 2

I've been feeling a little unsettled lately, like something isn't quite right. My nights have been plagued by these awful, inexpli-cable dreams that leave me feeling terror like no other.

I open my eyes and I am bound to a table; the thick leather straps dig painfully into my flesh, and I can barely move. Bright fluorescent lights obstruct my vision; the heat is intense, blistering my skin. A sweet, metallic scent lingers in the open air as my eyes adjust. I look down and my stomach swells and morphs; the skin stretches like an elastic band. The flesh tears in the middle and I am showered in crimson. From within, I watch a glistening, sinewy claw emerge. It's not long before I see its grotesque body, the skin a sickening slimy green. My intestines are woven around its neck. The shimmering, slick flesh oozes. It turns to look at me and for a moment, there is recognition, acknowledgment. It's Anna. She mouths words I cannot comprehend and then I wake up.

Entry 3

Anna is not my baby.

She's been… changing. I'd watch her in her cot late at night, her limbs swelling and contorting. Her tongue would writhe and distend in her mouth and her teeth… oh my god, her teeth. I'd see them in the dead of the night, wet and shiny, as sharp as daggers.

Entry 4

A few nights ago, I woke up with her at the foot of my bed. Her round little eyes were wild, bulging, burning into mine. I sat, frozen with fear. I asked what she wanted, "Soon, mamma." She told me.

What is she?

Final Entry

I open my eyes. Bright fluorescent lights blur my vision—a tangy, metallic smell hangs in the air like a corpse. I am bound to a table.

I look up and see a swollen figure standing before me; its olive-green skin shines and morphs in the light. I see scales, claws and razor-sharp nails shaped like coffins caressing my skin.

Someone is speaking. It sounds like a voice I know.

"It's ok, mother. It'll be over soon."

I hear another voice.

"Insemination complete."

THE SKINLESS CHILDREN

When I was a kid and right up until my late teenage years, I had this awful recurring dream. Each night, I'd dream about these five skinless children; their flesh would be on the outside, exposed and raw. They wouldn't do anything; they would just stand and stare at me—for hours and hours until I willed myself to wake up again. You see, these kids, they didn't have any faces; where their features were supposed to be, it was blank. There was nothing there. Just uncooked, jagged flesh. It looked smooth though, like I knew if I touched their faces, they would feel velvety and glossy.

That's fucked up, right?

Growing up, I could barely sleep for the fear of seeing their blank, nondescript, and bleeding faces again. My mum and dad would dismiss me when I'd tell them about it; my dad used to get particularly angry about it and I couldn't understand why. Each night, the dreams would become more surreal and vivid. The kids would appear more fucked up, somehow—sometimes they'd come to me with their skin still attached and they'd stand at the foot of my bed and peel bits off, like pieces of kebab meat.

Eventually, the lack of sleep and the constant, unrelenting terror messed me up so bad that I had to be put away, sectioned if you will. The strange thing was, though, as soon as I left my house—the dreams stopped. I was in the hospital for about 5 months before they released me; they boiled it down to some brief and momentary psychotic break. They gave me some pills to take and sent me on my merry way.

I returned home and continued with my life. My parents acted like nothing happened, of course. I left it at that. The first few days were normal, and I finally started to forget about those horrific dreams. Until one night. They appeared, and I wasn't asleep this time. I saw the familiar chunks of saw-edged flesh, wet and glistening. Their faces—blank. They stood at the foot of my bed and did something they had never done before.

They beckoned at me to follow them. I don't know why but I followed. They led me to the basement—I noticed that the lights were on. I gingerly walked down the steps into the dimly lit room and that was when I saw them all. There were five of them; the smell of their rotting corpses travelled up my nostrils, and the vomit erupted from within me, like blood from a freshly cut wound. They were skinned alive. Their faces were carved open. Noses, mouths and eyes were all gone, cut out.

I saw my father slashing and carving away at something.

He looked up and smiled at me.

"You were such a disappointment, son. The next one will be better."

Printed in Great Britain
by Amazon

47964400R00131